MR. DECEMBER

HEROES OF ROGUE VALLEY: CALENDAR
GUYS
BOOK 10

ANN ROTH

PUBLISHER'S NOTE: This is a work of fiction. Names, characters, places, and incidents either are the product of the author's imagination or are used fictitiously. Any resemblance to actual persons, living or dead, business establishments, events, or locales is entirely coincidental.

Copyright © 2018 Ann Roth

Published by Oliver-Heber Books

0 9 8 7 6 5 4 3 2 1

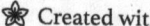 Created with Vellum

INTRODUCTION

Welcome to Ann Roth's exciting new series, Heroes of Rogue Valley: Calendar Guys series. *Ten months, 10 gorgeous firefighter heroes and the women who steal into their hearts and forever change their lives.*

Meet Mr. December:

Hurt by betrayal, firefighter Liam Gibson doesn't trust easily. The one time he let his guard down, photographer Grace Camry stole his heart. Liam intended to spend the rest of their lives together, until the unexpected death of Grace's father changed everything. Although Liam still harbors feelings for Grace, when she walked away without an explanation she shattered his trust.

Dad wasn't the man he seemed, and his lies and secrets almost destroyed Grace. Fearing the damage the truth would cause Liam, she ended the relationship. Yet she never stopped loving the firefighter with the big heart and amazing smile. Without him, her life seems colorless and empty.

Soon a holiday party for families in need will force them to work together and maintain a cordial front for the greater good. Will the past keep them apart, or will the magic of Christmas open their hearts to forgiveness and a new beginning?

Mr. December—Liam Gibson
  Age 30, 6'2" tall, 202 pounds
  Single
  Proud Senior Firefighter
  Time with Guff's Lake Fire Department: 8 years

Grace Camry was in the back room scrutinizing digital photos she'd taken at a silver wedding anniversary party when a faint buzzing sound signaled that someone had opened the door. Unexpected—for professional photographers, the day after Thanksgiving was typically dead, a brief calm before the flood of business from those who waited until it was almost too late to get photos for their Christmas cards. A surprising number of people procrastinated. With smart phone cameras, it was a wonder anyone still hired a professional, but they did. And thank goodness.

"Anyone here?" a man called out, his gruff voice permanently imprinted in her brain.

Liam Gibson. For a split second her heart lifted, but her flip-flopping stomach quickly overpowered that. They hadn't spoken since shortly after her father's death nearly sixteen months ago. Her choice, but she'd done what she had to.

What was he doing here?

"Coming," she answered, doing her best to hide her nervousness as she entered the front office.

He'd planted himself near the artificial Christmas tree, in front of a wall of photos, his large frame making the space seem even smaller than it was. Muscular, with a shaved head and the usual narrowed eyes and near snarl on his lips, he looked more like a World Wrestling Federation star than a firefighter. A worn leather jacket and a black bike helmet under his arm added to the "Don't screw with me" badass 'tude. Must've ridden the Harley today.

At one time that fierce expression had intimidated her. She knew now that underneath, Liam was a great guy, that when he liked and trusted someone enough to smile, his whole face lit up. He was also a fantastic lover. Remembering, her body perked up and started to tingle.

That was then, this is now.

He nodded, the furrows between his brows deepening. She fought the urge to wince. She deserved his scowl and more. "It's been awhile. Are you interested in a portrait?"

He shook his head. "The holiday party at Auntie's Place is in three weeks."

"You didn't have to stop by and remind me—I *am* the Guff's Like Fire Department photographer." The position had been offered to her when the fundraiser calendar she'd photographed and put together, featuring a different firefighter each month, had been a smashing success, going back to print twice and selling out every time.

She'd landed that job thanks to Liam's recommendation, back when life had been simpler. The higher-ups at the fire department had used her since then to photograph promotions, commendations, retirements, and other events. Yet until now, she'd managed to avoid Liam.

"Auntie's Place is a great organization," she added to cover the awkwardness. The community center served kids from low-income families. It provided child care and a safe place for teens to hang out, with after-school tutoring, nutritious snacks, and counseling services. "I volunteered to be a secret Santa to the kids in one family. I drew the names of two brothers. I have their wish list and I promised to keep my identity a secret forever."

"I do that every year. Anonymous works best, in case for some reason a problem arises."

Although Grace hadn't invited Liam to sit down, he shrugged out of the jacket, set it and his helmet on the low-slung table between the loveseat and chairs, then made himself comfortable on the loveseat. "How have you been?"

His eyes flitted over her pullover and pants, standard work attire in cold weather. She stifled the urge to tug the sweater over her hips. As if it mattered, when he knew every inch of her body intimately.

"I'm all right." She sat down across the table and nudged the candy bowl toward him.

If you didn't take into account her late father's betrayal and deception, and the consuming anger she felt toward him.

Acutely uncomfortable and needing to collect herself, she jumped up again. "Would you like a cup of coffee?"

"No, thanks."

"Well, I would. Excuse me."

She headed into the small kitchen adjacent to the back office and thought about the past. Fifteen months ago, a mere three weeks following a devastating diagnosis of advanced pancreatic cancer, Robert, as she'd referred to her father since she'd discovered who he really was, had passed on.

On his death-bed he'd apologized for his mistakes and wrongs. Thinking he felt bad for not letting her help him run RC Photography—he'd always been a bit of a control freak and claimed he wanted her to focus on honing her photographic skills—she'd said there was nothing to apologize for.

Little did she realize.

Knowing the business would soon be hers, he'd also extracted her tearful promise to protect his forty-year legacy as one of the top photographers in Guff's Lake. That had been easy. Robert was the best in the business, at least in the town of almost twenty thousand. People claimed Grace was just like him, with his eye and talent. She'd basked in the praise, her whole identity tied up with his. Such pride and respect for him.

Soon after his death she'd unearthed the mistakes and wrongs he'd alluded to, dark secrets neither she nor her mother had suspected. Debts, including a second mortgage on the house where Grace had grown up and where her mother still lived. He'd forged her mother's signature, which had forced her to take a second job or face foreclosure. The funds borrowed from a loan shark that had to be repaid within weeks or Grace would lose the business.

But his worst sin by far had been committed against Gil Booker, a widower and respected former firefighter who'd died an untimely death when his truck crashed head-on into a concrete wall. Alcohol had apparently been involved—a lot of it. Photos later found of Gil with a male lover suggested blackmail and possible suicide, but the police were unable to discover a money trail or determine the identity of the blackmailer. If they had, Robert would've gone to prison, and rightfully so. Grace had the negatives proving his culpability. Why he'd targeted Gil would remain a mystery forever.

"You okay?" Liam called out.

Hardly. "Still waiting for the coffee. I'll be there soon."

The driving force behind Robert stooping to such awful depths? The father Grace had worshipped for as long as she could remember, the man she'd trusted implicitly and completely, had turned out to be a gambling addict.

In hindsight, she wished she'd gone to the police immediately with the negatives. At the time, the shock of discovering he'd led a secret life for years had obliterated her judgment and doubled the pain of losing him, as well as shaken the foundations she'd built her life and career on.

And destroying her relationship with Liam.

Grace pulled her mug from the microwave. Coffee in hand, she returned to the front office. Liam was sucking a candy cane from the bowl, shifting it in his mouth with obvious relish, which for some reason made him very attractive. But then, everything about him was.

Returning to her seat, she cupped the mug between her hands and blew on it.

Gil Booker had been Liam's mentor and friend, and although he'd died well before Grace had met Liam, she couldn't tell him what her father must have done. The very thought of his reaction to the vile truth made her sick to her stomach. So she'd broken up with him and locked Robert's away dirty secrets where they belonged—in her heart.

Except for her mother, no one else knew and never would. They both agreed on that. Her promise to Robert aside, Grace was too ashamed.

Shame didn't stop the guilt that continued to eat at her.

She despised her father, yet missed him terribly. Harboring two conflicting feelings at the same time was confusing and upsetting, but she'd learned to live with that.

After a sip of coffee, she realized she didn't really want it and set it on the table between them.

The candy cane went still, and Liam fixed her with a probing but inscrutable expression. Unnerved, she helped herself to a candy cane. "How was your Thanksgiving?" she asked, peeling the cellophane back. "Did you spend it with your grandpa?" *And maybe your current girlfriend?*

He nodded. "Rafe and Jillian wanted to celebrate their first Thanksgiving as a married couple with a party. We ate there."

"They got married?"

"In October. Were you at your mom's?"

"For the entire day. Just us. We made a turkey and all the trimmings." Despite their shared anger and grief, they'd managed to enjoy themselves.

Enough with the small talk. She folded her hands in her lap. "I know you didn't come here just to say hello."

Liam sat up straight, his eyes slightly narrowed. "It's time we talked."

~

SINCE LIAM HAD last seen Grace, she'd lost weight and was too thin. He remembered the first day he'd laid eyes on her. The company where he moonlighted as a safety training instructor had hired her to take photos for a brochure advertising his class. Along with every other male in the room he'd noticed her long legs, big amber eyes, and curves. What had drawn him most was the openness that seemed to come easy to her, a rare thing in most people he knew, especially women. That and her can-do attitude had pretty much cinched his decision to ask her out.

Sitting across from her today, she looked like a different person. Circles under her eyes, gaze lowered, jittery foot.

Facing her wasn't any picnic for him either.

"Sixteen months ago, you said you needed time to grieve. I gave you the space you wanted. You took it and never looked back. You broke up with me on voice mail, for God's sake. 'I'm sorry and please don't contact me again' doesn't cut it. You ignored my voice messages and texts asking for an explanation, and you didn't answer when I stopped by your apartment building." He'd dropped by the studio too, but she never seemed to be in. "I deserve to know the truth."

The foot jiggled faster and she tugged a lock of her hair, another sure sign she was uncomfortable. "After all this time?"

He'd needed to wait until he was in a less emotional place so that he could face her calmly.

"You owe me. Plus, I want the kids and families at Auntie's Place to have fun, a few hours without unnecessary tension. We're both reasonable people, and we should be able to talk to each other like the adults we are. Let's clear the air so that we can relax when we're in the same room."

For the second time in fifteen minutes she pushed to her feet, as if she couldn't sit one more moment. She dropped the remnants of her candy cane in the trash, but remained silent.

It looked as if clearing the air was up to him. He stood to face her. "I thought we had a good thing going," he said softly. "You did too."

They'd been together five months—a record if you didn't count his short-lived marriage at twenty. In general, the women he'd been involved with tended to be less than candid about a whole host of things, some as insignificant as their natural hair color. Others, more serious, from hiding their true marital status to eating disorders. One had been a pathological liar.

Hell, his own mother had lied to him and his dad when she'd run off with "Uncle" Joe, a so-called family friend.

But Grace? The openness between them had been a breath of fresh air. Natural and comfortable, nothing phony. They didn't have to try to make their relationship work, it just did. She made him a better man, made him happy.

He'd always wanted a relationship based on trust and honesty. With her, he found it.

Within their first month together, he'd known he wanted to spend his life with her, build a family with kids, several of them. An only child herself, Grace wanted that too. She'd come with him to visit his grandpa several times, and Liam had eaten dinner at her parents'. They were good people, straight shooters like his grandfather, their love for each other and Grace a beautiful thing. Role models for the future he wanted with her.

Liam assumed they'd be together forever. But life had thrown him a curve ball. As determined as he was to forget Grace—and he'd dated several women since she'd walked away—he was still smarting from that. "I deserve to know what went wrong."

She stared at the floor. "Grief and running the business, which I'd never done before, while I worked with my own clients and Robert's, didn't leave time for anything else."

"You're calling him by his first name now?"

"It's easier."

Okay. Liam understood grief and the need to lose himself in something—for a while, booze, partying, and a marriage that had been a mistake from the get-go. "I've been there, remember? Both my parents died within a six-month span. Then my grandma, and a few years after that, Gil." Liam's mentor and friend had encouraged him to become a firefighter when he'd been aimless and lost.

Grace flinched as if the mention of so much loss hurt her physically. "I don't know how you survived." Biting her lip, she finally met his gaze. He saw pain and sorrow and a flash of anger. Then tears. "You never said how much it hurts."

He was also familiar with the outrage that followed the death of a loved one. Not long after his mother had taken off with Joe she'd changed her mind and ended the affair. On the drive back to Liam and his father, she'd died in a car accident, denying them the healing they all needed. So yeah, he knew about anger.

He reacted without a thought, pulling Grace close to comfort her just as he had when her father lay dying, and later, during and after the funeral. Holding her next to him felt good, like she belonged there. No other woman had ever fit him so well.

For the first time in way too long, he drew an easy breath. He kissed the top of her head, smelled the familiar sweet scent of her shampoo. She hated her unruly hair and spent a good deal of time straightening it most mornings, but the wayward curls weren't easily tamed.

They tickled his chin. He almost smiled, but didn't. Too many unanswered questions. Like why she'd grown distant within days after the funeral and dumped him.

He pulled away but Grace held on, her arms tight around him. "Please, Liam."

Warmth shimmered in her eyes, and her

mouth... Soft lips, lush and inviting. God help him, she was as impossible to resist as ever. "Please yes, or please no?" he growled.

"Yes."

He kissed her. More than once. The chemistry they'd shared from the start was alive and well, heat flaring and her lips as demanding as if she'd never ripped his heart in half.

He tore his mouth from hers. "We cool now?"

Blinking and looking anything but cool, she nodded.

He swung away from her, shrugged into his jacket, grabbed the helmet, and split.

2

S tanding out of view, Grace peered out the front window as Liam moved away from the studio. After days of gray, the weak winter sun had appeared, showering light on his massive shoulders and straight back. Helmet under one arm, stride long and confident, he exuded a raw strength she'd never been able to resist.

Was it any wonder she'd kissed him?

Correction: *he*'d kissed *her* after she'd begged him. *Brilliant, Grace.* The man had been involved with several women since they'd broken up— she'd kept tabs. Yet the second he'd touched her, nothing else had mattered but the here and now in his arms.

He was a block down the sidewalk now, but if she angled her head a certain way she could still see him. Powerful legs straddling the Harley Street 500 he loved, he strapped on his helmet and rode off.

She was still at the window when Marguerite, her best friend since middle school, waved and entered the studio with her golden doodle, aka Sexy Beast, straining at his leash. At the sight of Grace, Beast woofed and his rear end wriggled with excitement. Marguerite unhooked the leash and he raced toward Grace.

She leaned down to greet him, laughing when he licked her hand. "I love you too, you sweet thing."

"Don't call him that—you'll tarnish his manly dog image," Marguerite scolded with a smile. "I like the red and silver balls on your avocado tree and the evergreen sprigs along the windowsill and bookcase. They smell like Christmas. Nice touches, Grace."

Grace hadn't enjoyed Christmas in two years. For her, it was just another day to get through. But her clients expected a festive look and she'd done her part.

"Did I just see Liam Gibson ride off on his Harley?"

With a sigh, Grace nodded. "He stopped by to talk about the holiday party at Auntie's Place, the one the firefighters sponsor for families in need. That's a few weeks from now, and he wants everyone to have a good time. He thought we should clear the air now so that we'd be relaxed when I took pictures.

"He has nothing to worry about. After all, I'm

a professional. I would never let my personal life get in the way of a photo shoot."

"We're talking about Liam Gibson, the man who swept you off your feet before you broke up with him. As professional as you are, your history together could definitely affect your work." Her friend studied her. "If I had to guess, I'd say you kissed him."

Grace couldn't hide her surprise. "You can tell?"

"With your lips pinker than usual, your face flushed, and your hair a little wild... You look what a romance novelist would describe as 'thoroughly kissed.' "

"It wasn't planned."

"So he waltzes in, forgives you for ending the relationship, vows to win you back, takes you in his arms, and kisses you?"

Grace recalled his deep scowl and coolness toward her. "He didn't say anything about wanting me back, and I wouldn't say he's forgiven me. I doubt he ever will, but at least we talked. Anyway, he's moved on." Although the way he'd kissed her sure didn't feel that way. "He's been dating like crazy since we broke up."

"Which is exactly what you wanted him to do."

True, and she should have been relieved that he'd gotten over her so quickly. Was, but she didn't have to like it. "I shouldn't have kissed him. It won't happen again."

"That's too bad. Well, did you?"

"Did we what?"

"Clear the air."

After those kisses? If anything, life had just become more complicated. Grace didn't dare get close to him again. "I don't exactly know what we did. Anyway, I haven't loaded my equipment into the minivan yet," she said, changing the subject. "I'll do that now. Then we'll go."

Knowing it'd be a slow day, she'd offered to close the studio, drive into the Siskiyou foothills, and take Christmas photos of Marguerite and her dog among the evergreen trees. A nice change from the usual studio shoot, and a needed diversion from thoughts of Liam.

Her friend rubbed her hands together. "I'm so excited! You should see the matching Santa hats I bought for me and Beast."

"It's nice to see the sun for a change," Marguerite said as Grace pulled the minivan from the back alley where she'd parked it. "You picked a perfect afternoon for the shoot. A super cute guy came into the store the other day," she added. She managed Rogue Valley Cheesery, a specialty shop that sold locally made cheeses and all things cheese related.

"What's his name?"

"Zane. The same as the hero in a book I just read." Marguerite patted her heart. "With his green eyes and curly black hair, he could be on a book cover."

At times her friend could be so dramatic. Grace rolled her eyes. "He sounds cute. Did you flirt with him?"

"Of course. I also sold him cheese and a jar of wild huckleberry sauce to serve with it. For a wine and cheese party his sister invited him to."

"Cool that he and his sister are close. Did he ask for your number?"

"No, but I stuck my business card in the bag."

"Smart. I'll keep my fingers crossed."

"Back to Liam. What did you say to him?"

So much for taking her mind off the man. "That I'm still coping with the changes in my life and still learning the ropes of running the business."

Marguerite didn't know the truth about Robert, but she'd seen first-hand Grace's devastation and the overwhelming challenges of even getting out of bed in the months following his death, not always easy once she'd fully grasped the scope of her father's duplicity.

"You're doing much better than you were. If you and Liam start seeing each other again, you might even feel happy."

Not with the secrets and guilt pressing down. "We're not going to see each other."

"What a shame. He's so good-looking and such a great guy, better than all your previous boyfriends combined."

Grace couldn't argue with that. She'd had her share of boyfriends, but she'd never felt as close to anyone else, or been as turned on. A potent and irresistible combination.

"Imagine if you and Liam became a couple again in time for Christmas. The two of you sitting in front of a roaring fire, snuggling and sipping hot toddies..."

Marguerite launched into the rest of the scenario, sounding as if she were reading from a romance novel.

If only... For a few, blissful moments, Grace got sucked into the fantasy. Which was dangerous because it made her want what could never be.

Marguerite was still talking. "And then you'll get engaged and—"

"You heard me—Liam and I will never get back together."

"Why not?"

"Because he's moved on and so have I." Not yet, but she was trying. "Also, I'm not the same person I was before Robert died. I hope that kiss didn't give Liam the wrong idea."

On the off-chance it might, she needed to set him straight. Not on the phone, in person. Over the next few weeks she had a ton of photo shoots scheduled—holiday-themed pictures of families, couples, singles, and groups sure to replenish the empty business and personal bank accounts. She really couldn't spare the time to talk to Liam.

Never mind. She would make time, even if she had to force herself.

"What a pretty place for my photo." Marguerite pointed at a stand of evergreens with a small clearing in front.

Grace slowed to take a look at the perfect setting for a photo op. She'd been so distracted talking and thinking about Liam, she'd never even noticed. Pushing him from her thoughts, she pulled to the side of the road to set up.

FRESH AIR always cleared Liam's head, especially cold air. Feeling at loose ends Sunday, he rode the Harley into the foothills. Likely the last time until spring, as the snow was bound to hit soon.

His crewmate Tony lived up here, but he was preoccupied with Summer and the baby they were expecting in a few weeks. Liam wasn't in the mood for company anyway. He needed to straighten himself out, stop thinking about Grace.

Who was he kidding? He hadn't stopped thinking about her since the night she'd showed up at his class with her camera. Most of the time when he set his mind to do something, he made it happen. Where Grace was concerned, not so easy. Forgetting her was a priority, and he fought himself daily to move on. He'd been making decent headway—until he'd walked into her studio the other day.

She'd knocked him out with those kisses. He was still aroused. And pissed off about it.

Of all the lamebrain things to do. Had he lost his marbles?

Pretty much, once she'd teared up and hugged him.

When they'd been a couple, they'd spent most Sundays together. Going out for brunch, taking rides on the Harley, Grace pressed against his back with her arms around his waist. Speeding through the foothills and touring Oregon. Making love everywhere, including on a blanket out here. The sex always leaving him hungry for more.

Loving her, fusing his body and soul with hers, had been the deepest experience of his life. He'd never felt a connection like that before or since, had never realized what had been missing all his life. He wanted to find it again.

Kinda hard to do when she'd stirred up feelings from before.

Tired of his walk down memory lane, he set his jaw, pushed her from his thoughts, and sped up until the whipping wind drowned out everything but the rolling hills. When the punishing cold numbed his face, he headed home. Unfortunately, as soon as he parked the bike in the garage, his thoughts returned to Grace.

Inside, he warmed up with steaming coffee and headed for the basement, where he took his frustrations out on the punching bag. Then a hot shower.

The Santa suit he'd rented for the party at Auntie's Place was hanging in the closet in his bedroom, in a protective clothing bag. He'd picked it up yesterday, minutes before the rental shop closed, and hadn't had time to try it on. He needed to see if it fit and if it didn't, to exchange it before the store closed this afternoon. Otherwise, he wouldn't make it back until after his double shift ended Wednesday. By then, the rest of the suits could easily be rented out.

After he dressed he tried it on over his jeans and a flannel shirt. The Santa jacket's sleeves were about an inch and a half too short, and the belly area too roomy, although a pillow might help. The pants barely reached the tops of his ankles. For kicks, he put on the white wig, beard, and Santa hat. In his socks, he padded to the spare bedroom opposite the master, which contained the only full-length mirror in the house. He looked ridiculous.

Wouldn't you know, the doorbell rang. Of all the...

From the window, he peered down to see who it was. Grace. What the hell?

He headed downstairs at a rapid clip, pulling off the hat and fake hair on the way and tossing them on the living room couch.

She was turning to leave when he opened the door. "Hey," he said.

"Liam, I—" She stopped and widened her eyes. "Look at you."

"Pretty hot duds, huh?"

She bit back a smile. Grinning—because what other option was there?—he gestured her inside. "I was trying this on to check the fit," he said as he closed the door behind her.

"I don't think it's your size."

"Nope."

"Although..." Standing in the entry with slightly narrowed eyes, she studied him as if he were the subject of one of her photos. "If you put a throw pillow under that coat it could work. And add a hat and beard."

"I have those and a wig."

"Put them on."

"Okay, but don't laugh." In the living room all decked out, he waited for the verdict. "Well?"

Trying hard not to laugh, eyes twinkling, she pulled her cell phone from her purse. "I have to take a picture of this."

"You do, and I may have to kill you."

The warning was barely out before she cracked up. A contagious sound impossible to ignore.

Howling with glee, she doubled over.

His own grin growing, he shed the hat and hair. Pretty soon they were both laughing so hard, neither of them could speak, clutching each other to keep from falling over.

After some time, they both settled down.

Stepping back, Grace wiped her eyes. "I haven't laughed like that in forever. It felt good."

"Ditto." Another thing he'd missed when they'd broken up—frequent laughter. He took off the coat, stepped out of the pants, and gestured her toward a chair. "What brings you here?"

Shaking her head, she remained standing. "I don't plan to stay long. About the other day... What we did... You're seeing other women and I'm swamped with work and a lot has happened and there's so much to do and take care of with no end in sight and—"

"Slow down, Grace. Just say what you mean."

"I was rambling, wasn't I? What I wanted to say in my roundabout way is, I don't want you getting the wrong idea about us kissing. I don't think we should get back together."

"That makes two of us."

He never wanted to get back with her. Instead of leaning on him in her time of pain and grief and God knew else what she felt, she'd pushed him away, when a true partnership between a man and a woman meant sticking together through thick and thin. His mother had done the same thing during a rough patch with his father, turning to Joe to escape from their marital problems instead of working through them.

Grace seemed both relieved and disappointed. Weird, but women often confused him.

"Phew. I should've known. I mean, you've dated a lot since we broke up."

The second mention she'd made of him and other women since she'd stepped into the house. Almost as if she'd kept tabs on him. He frowned. "How do you know I've been dating?"

"I hear things. You know, from Wanda when I get my hair cut, or when I run into any of the women I met through the fire department."

Wives and girlfriends of some of Liam's crewmates. "What did you expect me to do, sit around and mope?"

She stiffened. "Of course not. I was surprised it happened so quickly after we broke up, that's all."

"It wasn't that fast." It'd taken months before he could look at another woman, and he never dated the same one more than a few times. The fit always seemed off.

"Answer me this. Do you have a girlfriend now?"

"If I did, do you think I would have kissed you the other day?"

Her eyebrows shot up. "I offended you."

"Damn straight. You know me better than that. When I'm with someone, I don't kiss anyone else."

"That's true. I don't know why I asked." She tugged at a lock of her hair. "That's what I came here to say. I have to get home—you wouldn't believe all the work I have to finish today, or the busy week I have scheduled."

And he needed to get to the costume rental

store before it closed. "You drove all the way over here to tell me you don't want to get back together." She nodded. "You could've saved yourself the trip and phoned instead."

"I wanted to say it in person. Which I should have done when we broke up. I'm sorry I didn't."

He appreciated that. "You were pretty torn up —you couldn't think straight. We all make mistakes. I sure have."

Like letting his defenses down as soon as he met Grace when he knew better. He didn't trust people until they proved themselves. With her, he'd skipped right over that. A lapse that had earned him a hard kick in the chest.

And a solid reminder not to do it again.

"Still, it was inconsiderate. I didn't know what else to do."

"You did what you thought you needed to at the time."

"Yes, but I should have..." She broke off with a guilty look, as if she'd revealed too much. "Never mind."

He sensed she was hiding something from him. "Now you're going to argue against yourself." He scoffed. "Or is there something I need to know?"

She didn't answer that. "I always did talk too much."

"I never thought so."

They shared a long look, filled with meaning and blame and things better left unsaid. She blinked first. She wanted to leave and he wanted to get to the costume rental place.

"While you're here, I may as well show you the upstairs remodel." Anyone's guess why he'd thought up a reason for her to stay.

"I wondered how that turned out."

Better than he'd imagined. Grace's input had helped a lot, her ideas pushing his own to new levels. The architect and construction company had implemented most of them. "See for yourself. You may want to take off your coat and scarf before you roast to death."

She laid her things on the back of the couch. She *would* be wearing snug jeans and a hot pink sweater that clung to her breasts. He gestured her up the stairs, following a few steps behind, his eyes on her shoulder bag, bumping her sweet rear end.

As she reached the second floor she stopped cold. Eager to see her reaction, Liam hurried to stand beside her.

"Oh, Liam—an octagonal room, windows all around, just like we talked about," she said, sounding wowed as she started toward the room. "This changes the entire upstairs. Even on an overcast day like today, there's so much light, and not just in here. The hallway is brighter too."

Her comments pleased him. "I like to call it my light room. The gloomy little rooms that used to be here are long gone."

She wandered around the new space. "You even added a gas fireplace. It's beautiful."

With her face lit up, so was she. But for his own good, she was off-limits. He stepped away, out of reach. "Sometimes after dinner I turn the fireplace on and leave the other lights off. Then it's a whole different space, and pretty damn spectacular."

She dropped her purse to the floor. "I'll bet. Day or night, I don't see how you can ever leave," she said, absently caressing the extra-long leather couch he'd special ordered for the space while she gazed through the window at the Siskiyous in the distance.

He knew that loving touch up close and personal. With its usual hunger, his cock twitched and started to rise. He cleared his throat. "I spend a lot of time here when I'm home."

"Seeing your plans realized is a real treat. Thanks for showing me." She walked backward as if she couldn't tear her gaze away from the view and bumped smack into him. His bad for getting mesmerized by her swaying hips.

"Sorry," she said.

"No problem." Instead of moving away like the smart man he was, he wrapped his arms around her from behind. She didn't stop him.

He brought her closer and she swiveled her head to stare up at him, her lips so close he could bend down and...

He caught the responding desire in her eyes

before she looked straight again. "We shouldn't, Liam."

"Yeah, but we want to." Smoothing her hair away from her ear, he pulled on the lobe with his teeth.

She moaned. "Why did you do that?"

"Because you like it. You always did."

"I do not."

"Uh-huh." He nibbled the sweet spot where her neck and shoulder met and she leaned against him.

"We're *not* getting back together."

He nibbled again. "We don't have to be a couple to fool around."

"That's a good point, but I need to think about it." She arched her back, thrusting her breasts out and pushing her soft rear end against his erection.

"Think away." He slid his hands up her ribcage, stopping a finger's distance from her nipples.

She went very still. So did he, although his fingers twitched. Along with his cock. She had to feel him lengthen and thicken. She let out an exaggerated sigh. "Oh, all right."

"All right what?"

She pivoted in his arms. "Let's fool around."

With a soft laugh he walked her backward to the couch.

3

Pressed up close to Liam on his rich leather sofa, Grace tried to reason with herself. She shouldn't be sitting here, her lips glued to his like he was her sole air support. This was dangerous, reckless, foolish.

She had to stop!

But with his tongue exploring her mouth and his skilled thumbs teasing her nipples, her logic faded in a haze of desire. She needed him, needed this, too much to struggle with herself. As long as they stuck to physical only, everything would be fine.

She wanted his hands on her bare skin, to take off her pullover. As if he'd read her mind, or maybe because he knew her well, he tugged it over her head, then unbuttoned his shirt and tossed it aside. She'd never tired of looking at his bare torso. "You have the best body ever," she murmured, unable to resist running her hands down his honed pecs and abs.

He groaned, and her bra joined her sweater on the floor. He pushed her onto her back and had his wicked, delicious way with her breasts, giving her pleasure she'd gone without for such a long time. She was restless and moaning and ready to climax against the powerful thigh thrust between her legs when her cell phone rang.

"Dammit," she muttered. "Ignore that."

"It could be a client."

He sat up, then stood and retrieved her purse. Covering her breasts with her arm, which was ridiculous when he'd seen her naked countless times, she pulled out her cell and frowned at the screen. "It's my mother. I don't want to talk to her now."

But the thought of her mom and the shameful secrets they shared doused the fire burning inside.

She scooped her bra and sweater from the floor and held them to her chest. "I'm sorry, Liam. I can't do this right now."

As she dressed, Liam put on his own shirt and buttoned it up.

At the front door, he held her coat while she slipped into it. He gave her a last, quick kiss, then opened the door. As she headed out, she gave a good-bye wave.

～

"I DID A CRAZY THING," Liam said Monday over breakfast in the firehouse kitchen. "I saw Grace Friday."

Rob look dumbfounded. "On purpose?"

"Yep. I stopped by the photography studio." All eleven crewmates stared at him with wide eyes. "I was in the area and figured we should talk," he explained. "To cut down on tension and confusion before I see her at Auntie's Place."

"Considering you haven't seen each other since you broke up, that must've been tense," Rob agreed.

Tony winced. "Those kinds of conversations are never fun."

"This one sure was interesting," Liam said. "We didn't stop at talking."

Ethan shook his head. "Don't tell me you're sleeping with her again."

"Nah—a kiss or two." Even that had incinerated his smarts.

Rob gaped at him. "Are you nuts?"

"Hey, man, cut him some slack," Rafe advised. Recently married, with Jillian newly pregnant, nothing fazed him.

"What Rafe said," Max chimed in. "It's tough to ignore a woman when you still have feelings for her. Which Liam does."

Liam glared at them all. "Do you want to hear about this or not?" They shut up and he went on. "That was Friday. Sunday, she dropped by my place—big surprise to me—and apologized for the way she dumped me."

"About damn time," Rob said. "Nice touch that she did it to your face."

"She also made it clear that she doesn't want to get back together. I told her I don't either. I showed her the remodel, then we fooled around."

"You're going to sleep with her." Ethan raised his eyebrows. "What kind of game are you playing?"

"I'm not worried. This is a physical thing."

"Sure about that?"

"After the hell she put me through?" Liam had zero interest in going there again. He had his standards. Fool me once, et cetera. He changed the subject. "I have Laundromat news."

Some years ago, his grandfather had started a side business, opening Gibson Laundromat, He'd soon expanded. Now there were three Laundromats. Way back when, before Liam had met Gil, he'd been adrift and grief-stricken after losing his parents and the subsequent failure of his short-lived marriage. His grandpa had hired him to manage the Laundromats. Recently, Liam had bought him out.

"And the Laundromat saga continue." Rob eyed him. "Which supervisor quit this time?"

"Shut your mouth. Employment is stable at all three locations. This is good news. It's official —I'm expanding."

"You won the bid on that old Laundromat near Guff's Lake Resort?"

"Yep. My Realtor called last night."

"Congrats. That's a prime location, but the place is a dump."

"It won't be after the remodel. I'll have to close for a while, but I figure I'll get my investment back within three to four months."

"Or sooner." Tony whistled. "With tourism higher than ever and growing, and the cabins at the resort at full capacity, you'll make a mint."

"Exactly. I want the remodel finished by early spring. Once I start turning a profit, I'll donate ten percent to the Mentoring Project." Which was the non-profit Liam and several retired fire-fighters had founded after Gil's death, for the purpose of mentoring fatherless kids.

"Cool," Rob said. "Are you going to do the work yourself?"

"Some. The rest I'll hire out. The wiring will be updated late next week, and the plumber comes a few days later. The rest of the contractors I'll need are booked until January. Meantime, I could use a hand gutting the place."

Rafe, Nate, and Rob volunteered to help.

They were cleaning up the lunch mess when the alarm sounded. Dispatcher Sarah McCone directed them to a house fire in the foothills, not far from where Liam had taken the Harley Sunday.

It was a two-fire truck call, Nate at the helm of

one truck, Liam the other. Due to freezing rain the roads were slippery, and he drove as fast as safety allowed, arriving seconds ahead of the other truck to find flames licking at the second floor and roof of the house. Outside, a mother and three kids under the age of four huddled together with neighbors. The father, having rushed home from work, arrived soon after.

While crewmates from both trucks battled the fire, Liam and Tony rescued an aging mixed-breed dog and two parakeets. Then they joined the other firefighters. By the time they'd extinguished the blaze, extensive damage had made the home unlivable.

Tearful and grateful that no one was hurt, the distraught homeowners wondered where they would go. Kind neighbors offered to take the family in, and Liam directed them to the Firefighters' Benefit Fund, which existed to provide financial assistance to fire victims.

"Bitch of a fire," Liam commented to the crew members in his truck, Max, Tony, and Owen, as he navigated the narrow road descending the foothills.

Owen touched his biceps and shoulder, the sites of recently healed scars caused by burns sustained during a summer fire, and blew out a breath. "Thank God no one was hurt."

"That fire could've been easily prevented if the family had understood the dangers of overloading a two-plug outlet with multiple surge protectors," Liam added. "I think that deserves a mention in my safety training class."

His crewmates seconded the idea. The rest of the drive they rehashed the details between lengthy silences. Liam's adrenaline was still pumping when he pulled into the apparatus bay.

The remainder of the day passed uneventfully. In bed that night, he lay awake. He'd never made it to the costume rental place Sunday afternoon, but he'd contacted the store. As he'd suspected, there weren't many Santa costumes left. The clerk who answered the phone promised to hold one of the remaining costumes for him to try on. He agreed to stop by on his way to class Wednesday.

Whether or not he found a better fit, he wouldn't trade the afternoon with Grace. Hands under his head, he relived every sigh and moan, and wondered when he'd see her again. They were both busy, but with their chemistry they'd find a way. Finally, he fell asleep.

Before he knew it, his double shift ended. After breakfast with several crewmates at Rosemary's Breakfast Nook, their favorite haunt Wednesday mornings, he went home and figured out a way to fit in a lesson about extension cords during tonight's class.

Then he conked out for a few hours. When he woke up, he had just enough time to exchange the Santa costume before class. He headed for the rental store, where the woman who'd offered to hold a costume for him retrieved it. She was friendly and about his age, with red hair and pretty eyes. He tried it on for her.

She didn't hide her interest in him. "It fits," she said, with a warm smile. "But you need padding. How about a fake belly?"

He added that to his order. After making the exchange, she handed him her business card and wrote her cell phone number on it. He considered getting together with her, but meh. At the moment, he was interested in Grace. Physically only.

As he laid the Santa suit and padding in the back seat of the Yukon, a sedan pulled in beside him with a friendly honk. Curious, he glanced over. Grace's mom was staring at him.

4

Liam hadn't seen Grace's mother since the funeral. Same amber eyes and smile as Grace, but Grace had inherited her father's curly brown hair. He greeted her with a nod. "Hey, Diane."

"Hello, Liam." In the cold air, her breath plumed like cigarette smoke. She managed a shaky smile, no doubt still laid low by her husband's death. "I think often of the flowers you sent. You were so thoughtful."

"As was your thank-you note." Grief aside, the woman seemed tired and worn down. "How are you doing?"

"Feeling a little crazed. I've taken a second job at General Hardware, and sometimes I don't know whether I'm coming or going." She pointed to the large building that shared the parking lot with other retailers.

"I thought you worked full time at Rogue Valley Middle School."

"That's right."

He figured she wanted a full plate. Not a bad way to cope with loss. Better than drinking and partying and getting married, then divorcing six months later like he'd done.

"Are you going to the hardware store?" she asked.

He shook his head and told her about the Santa costume and his upcoming class.

"You're busy too."

"Always. I saw Grace the other day."

Her sudden wary expression didn't make sense. "Oh?"

"She seems all right."

"We're both managing." A gust of icy wind whipped around them, and Diane pulled the lapels of her coat together. "I forgot my scarf. Didn't I tell you my life is insane?"

"I might have a spare in the Yukon, if you'd like to borrow it."

"That's all right. I've always liked you, Liam. I want you to know that."

Okay. "Same. I liked Robert too."

Something shifted in her expression. It wasn't grief. She checked her watch. "If I don't hurry, I'll be late. So nice to see you."

"You too. Take care."

She hurried away. Call it a gut feeling, but he sensed she was hiding something, the same as Grace. Their business, unless it concerned him. But finding out would be good, especially if it shed light on the breakup. Something he'd mention to Grace next time he saw her.

The idea stayed with him and wouldn't let go even while he taught the safety class. He needed to know now. After class, he'd planned to go home. Instead, he drove to Grace's apartment building.

AFTER FOUR PHOTO SHOOTS, three for Christmas cards and one for a "save the date" wedding announcement, Grace was ready to go home and relax for the evening once she finished up at the studio. Selecting half a dozen photos from each shoot, cropping and fiddling with the lighting and backgrounds to highlight the subjects in the most flattering ways, emailing the proofs to her clients to rank in order of preference, then creating files of the final selections for printing took a fair amount of time and effort.

Her favorite shoot of the day featured an adorable seven-month-old laughing baby and a well-behaved Vizsla stretched out on a fluffy rug in front of one of the trees she used for Christmas photo sessions. The pictures of the young couple decorating another tree weren't bad, either. They'd brought their own ornaments, a nice touch. The extended family of eight needed extra TLC, since catching them all looking happy at the same time proved challenging.

Every photo made her think of Liam. At one time, they'd planned to marry and have a big family. He was lucky, though—he considered his crewmates family and also still had his grandpa. Grace had her mother, period. And of course, Marguerite. At least she and her mom didn't have to hide the humiliation and shame Robert had stuck them with from blood relatives.

She'd enjoyed their time together Sunday, but being with Liam also made her sad for what she'd given up when she'd said good-bye to him. The laughter and they kisses they'd shared made her heartache as fresh and painful as if it had happened yesterday.

If only her father had been the man she'd believed he was... But he'd lied and hurt the people he supposedly loved, and there was no going back.

Shortly before seven, she finally finished. Starving and eager to get home and eat, she quickly sorted through the day's mail. A few Christmas cards and a stack of bills, ninety percent of them related to the mountain of debt Robert had saddled her with. Digging out from under that seemed like a never-ending struggle. Would she ever get there?

The phone rang. Her mother. They were both extremely busy and hadn't seen each other or spoken since Thanksgiving a full week earlier. Also, maybe Grace didn't want to tell her about

Liam. Putting a smile in her voice, she answered. "Hi, Mom. I'm just closing up shop."

"I called you Sunday."

"Your voice message said not to call back," Grace said.

"Because I know you're swamped. I won't keep you long—I'm on dinner break and I only have a few minutes left."

"It's Thursday, remember? You work Monday, Tuesday, and Wednesday."

"Not since they asked me to add Thursdays and Saturdays."

"On top of your full-time job? That's a lot. No wonder you sound tired."

"It's only through New Year's and I need the money. Besides, winter break starts in two weeks. I'm so ready for that."

Her mother having to take the second job was Robert's doing, and was taking a toll. If he were still alive, Grace would've strangled him. "Did you have time to eat?" she asked, hiding her anger.

"Over the weekend, I made a pot of turkey soup. I brought it in a Thermos for dinner."

"Yum. You sure are tough."

"So are you. I ran into Liam earlier. He was leaving that costume rental place near the hardware store. He said he'd seen you."

So much for not mentioning him to her mom. "That's right."

"Why didn't you tell me?" Her mother sounded hurt or maybe nervous.

"This is the first time you and I have talked since then."

"Are you seeing him again?"

"No." That wasn't a lie. Twice and a few sizzling kisses didn't count as "seeing" him.

"Do you want to?"

"Don't, Mom."

"He misses you."

"I know he didn't tell you that."

"I have eyes. You should've seen the look on his face when he mentioned you."

Grace knew she'd hurt him. She hurt too. Like a scar ripped open, the ache she'd fought since she'd broken up with him filled her heart. "Stop it."

"It's a shame you had to break up with him."

"I didn't have a choice, did I?"

Time and distance hadn't dimmed her feelings one bit. Although she'd never used the L word with Liam—she'd been waiting for him and had assumed that sooner or later he'd say it—she'd loved him then and still did.

When things had been different, that love had made her heart sing on the darkest days. Now... She swallowed back a sob. If only he hadn't stopped by the other day. Didn't she have enough to deal with?

"Can't you see him without telling him what your father did?" her mother asked.

"Could *you* keep a secret like ours from the man you loved?"

"Your father loved me and you, and he kept a lot from us," her mother said in her "I'm getting upset" voice. "He fooled me and he fooled you, and I can't even slap his face."

The pain and anger Grace heard in her mom's voice echoed her own. "And we pay for his lies and secrets every day of our lives," she said, not hiding her bitterness. "Sometimes I wish I'd never picked up a camera or made him a promise."

"You don't mean that, Grace. Photography is in your blood and you're very good at it. As for the promise, your father's reputation and legacy are hard earned and have nothing to do with his lies or the crimes against poor Gil Booker."

Good points. Grace loved her chosen career and couldn't imagine doing anything else. In that respect, as she'd heard from clients and others who'd known her father, the apple hadn't fallen far from the tree.

Talented by birthright and tainted by association. She grimaced.

Did her mom ever wish they'd told the police about the blackmail? Grace didn't dare voice the question. At the moment, her mother was too upset.

"Our only saving grace is that no one but us knows the terrible burdens we live with," her mother added. "I couldn't bear for anyone else to know. It's too shameful."

Her voice had risen to full-fledged drama,

shaking and filled with unshed tears. Striving for a calm she didn't feel, Grace said, "I'm right there with you, Mom. We both need to take deep breaths and push ahead. I guess I needed to vent, and you're the only person I can do it with."

She inhaled and exhaled twice before her mother replied. "It's good that you let it out, honey." She almost sounded like her normal self. At least one of them had calmed down. "Duty calls —my dinner break is over. Love you."

"Love you, too."

Angry and sad, Grace drove home on autopilot. She poured herself a glass of wine, sipping it while she made dinner. She helped herself to a second glass and enjoyed it while she ate in front of the TV and watched a Christmas movie.

Which was supposed to cheer her up, but didn't. In Christmas movies, the characters solved their problems by the end of the film, the hero and heroine having overcome the obstacles to their happiness just in time to celebrate.

If only real life was like that.

It wasn't. People betrayed each other. They had secrets they didn't dare share, terrible secrets that drove wedges between them.

This was Grace's second Christmas without her father. Both had been mere shells of previous years' festivity and fun. Last year had been spent in grief and ignorance of the blackmail and financial mess he'd caused. This year's theme was anger.

She glanced around her tidy apartment. Not a shred of the holiday here.

Christmas was for people who believed in miracles, but miracles didn't exist. Bah humbug.

Her emotions had left her spent and unhappy. Ready to crawl into bed and sleep away the blues, she did her bathroom thing. As she returned her toothbrush to its holder, the security phone in the kitchen rang, announcing a visitor. At almost ten? Frowning, she headed for the kitchen and pushed the intercom button. "Yes?"

"It's Liam."

Of all times for him to show up. "It's late. I'm in my pajamas."

"Won't be the first time I've seen you like that. Can I come up?"

"All right." She buzzed him in, then rushed to put on her robe.

5

Liam strode across the lobby of the aging brick building where Grace lived and rode the elevator to the third floor. Finding her door open a fraction, he stepped into the tiny entry and shut the door. "Honey, I'm home," he called out.

"You're such a cut-up." She came out from the living room wearing fuzzy pink socks and a burgundy ankle-length robe.

She hadn't been kidding about being ready for bed. He greeted her with a quick kiss. "You smell like wine."

"I've had a few glasses. I needed to unwind."

"I know the feeling. I like those socks and the robe. You look cute."

"Not as cute as you did in that Santa costume." Her lips twitched.

"Don't remind me. I exchanged it for another that fits better. Living room or kitchen?"

She gave him a curious look. "Tell me again why you're here."

He needed answers to the questions rattling around in his head, but his gut warned him to ease into the subject. "I taught a class tonight, and didn't feel like going straight home. Here I am."

"How about the living room. After I get more wine. Care to join me?"

"Sure." He followed her down the hall. "I always liked this kitchen."

"Why? It's small and dated."

"I'd call it vintage. It feels comfortable and reminds me of the kitchen at the house where I grew up." When life was normal and his parents were relatively happy.

"Really? You never said anything before."

"I didn't think about it until now." He'd been too consumed with Grace. Lucky thing he was past all that.

"I'm glad you have good memories."

"More or less. My parents loved each other and treated me well, but we both know how lonely being an only child is. With no siblings to deflect some of the attention, the pressure can be overbearing at times."

"That's so true." Looking sick at heart, Grace filled two glasses, passed one to Liam, and took a sip from hers.

Clearly she was hurting, no doubt missing her father. Liam's chest constricted. After ten years, he still missed both his parents. Also Gil, who'd been a surrogate father and had steered him into firefighting. If not for his friendship and advice, no telling where Liam would be now. He couldn't imagine doing anything else and owed the man so much.

"I bought another Laundromat," he said.

"That's four. You're building an empire."

"A very small one. This place needs work. I'll be spending the next couple of days tearing off the drywall and hauling away the old washers and dryers."

"Working at the fire department and teaching class doesn't keep you busy enough?"

"Nope."

Figuring Grace would join him, he took a seat on the living room couch. Instead, she plunked into the armchair across the coffee table. "You haven't decorated for Christmas," he noted.

"Not in two years."

Everything he said seemed to make her blue. Probably shouldn't have stopped by, but too late now. He nodded at the upright piano against the wall. "Still taking lessons?"

She shook her head. "I've been too busy to even think about that. It's sadly out of tune. How was your class?"

"Pretty good. I added a new piece about outlet and extension cord safety."

He told her about the fire. "That family lost their home and nearly all their possessions. If they'd known the hazards of overburdening a circuit and had used a few simple safety precautions, they'd still have their home today."

"I feel so sorry for them," Grace said. "Here in the apartment, I don't have anything like that, but the studio is another story. I'd disconnect some of the extension cords and surge protectors if I could, but it's an old building and I don't have enough outlets as it is."

"Promise me you'll disconnect them anyway and get the wiring updated."

Muttering about the expense involved, she pushed her hair behind her ears. "This is one of my busiest seasons. I can't be without power sources."

Liam frowned. "I get that, but it's dangerous. Hey, why don't I stop by tomorrow before business hours and come up with something safer? What time is your first appointment?"

"Nine-thirty."

"I'll be there at eight."

She wrinkled her nose. "That's earlier than I'd like, but you're wearing your stubborn face, and I know what that means—I don't have a choice."

"Not when you're exposing yourself to a possible fire hazard."

"All right, I'll meet you there at eight a.m. But don't expect me to be a bright-eyed ball of energy."

"Good." That settled, he sat back. "I ran into your mom this afternoon."

"She called earlier and told me. She asked a lot of questions."

"About?"

"You. Us."

"What did you tell her?" he asked, giving her a sideways look.

"The truth—that we're not seeing each other."

"You don't call fooling around seeing each other?"

"I meant in the traditional sense—dating and spending time together doing things besides making out." She raised her eyebrows. "Is that why you're here tonight, for more of what we did at your house?"

That sounded good to Liam, except... "That wasn't my intention. You seem tired, but if you want to, I'm game."

"I'm not in the mood. You're right about me being tired. So far this has been a hectic week, with no end in sight until a few days before Christmas. Everyone wants their holiday photo yesterday."

"No wonder you're stressed. Are you keeping up?"

"Barely. Mom, though... She's doing too much." Grace set her empty wine glass on a coaster on the table.

"Two jobs, one of them full-time." Liam shook his head. "When you're grieving, you do what you need to survive. Staying busy helps."

"To a certain extent." Grace sucked on her

bottom lip and studied her hands, locked together in her lap.

Time for answers. "She gave off weird vibes, like she was hiding something from me," Liam said. "Similar to the vibes you gave off that day I stopped by the studio."

"I did?"

Her hard swallow and guarded expression confirmed his suspicions. "Something has you and your mom spooked, and I can't shake the feeling that it has to do with me."

"It's not about you, Liam, I swear." She centered the glass on the coaster.

"Say that and look me in the eyes."

She raised her troubled gaze and pulled on a lock of her hair, straightening it. Then she let go and it curled again. "This has nothing to do with you."

He believed her, but couldn't shake the feeling that something was missing from the story. "Ah, your dad," he guessed. "Christmas can be a rough time."

"That's pretty much it."

"I feel your pain. As time passes, it'll get better, although the hole they leave never goes away."

She squeezed her eyes shut as if fighting back tears. Wishing he could ease her pain, he stood, rounded the coffee table, and pulled her to her feet. "You look like you could use a hug."

"I so could."

She stepped into his open arms and he pulled her close. Despite the warm room and her robe, her hands were ice cold. She wrapped her arms around his waist, clutching him like she would a life preserver if she'd fallen into the middle of Guff's Lake and were desperate not to drown.

The same as she had when her father lay dying, and later at the funeral and the days that followed. She'd needed him, clung to him, absorbing his strength and comfort. Then suddenly she'd changed, pulling away without warning and no explanation. Why?

He couldn't think about that now. Grace was hurting, and tonight he would do what he could to comfort her.

Acting purely on instinct, he led her to the couch and tugged her onto his lap. He kissed the top of her head and smelled her shampoo. Beneath that, the faint woman scent that always sent him over the edge.

Tonight, his lust took a back seat to her wants and needs. With a sigh, she nestled closer and somehow curled into him. Physically, and also in a visceral way. Taking root in his soul again. Not that he'd ever been able to push her out. His chest expanded with tenderness and feelings he didn't want.

Falling for her again was not an option, and dammit, holding her like this was dangerous. He released her, or tried. Refusing to let go, she raised her head.

Those amber eyes... Bright and filled with too many emotions to read. Cupping her beautiful face in his hands, he kissed her. Very gently. "Whatever you need, I'm here for you."

He'd meant his words to assure and comfort her, but they seemed to cause more pain. Man, that sucked. "What is it, Gracie?"

The look on her face—sweet and bleak at the same time. "You haven't called me that in ages."

Not since they'd broken up. "It slipped out. Does it bother you?"

She studied her thumb and shook her head. "I like it," she said in a voice so soft, he wondered if he'd misheard.

If he hadn't been holding her, he'd have missed the fine tremors running through her rigid muscles. Her suffering hurt him. "You're awful tense," he said.

"I thought the wine would help, but it isn't working."

"I know what you need—a foot massage."

At last, a tremulous smile. "When did you become a mind reader?"

He grinned. "I know you, remember? Both socks off, then scoot against the arm rest."

When she was settled, her back propped up in the corner of the couch and her legs out straight, he set her bare feet on his thigh. "Your feet are freezing. I'll warm them up in no time."

After opening the bottom half of her robe and rolling her flannel pajama bottoms up to her

knees, he started on her toes, massaging each
and every one.

"That feels so good." She sighed and sagged in
relief. The lapels of the robe gaped open, exposing a hint of one breast against her pajama tee.

That he could do this for her filled him with
satisfaction. And lust. Yep, his hunger was alive
and raging. Always had been when he touched
her. Focus. He didn't trust himself to speak while
he worked. Soon she was limp and breathing
easy. "All warm now," he said, giving both feet a
reassuring squeeze but not ready to let her go.

He set to work on her calves. She groaned.
"You always did know how to work magic with
your fingers."

"They like making you happy."

"Could you go a little higher up?"

"How high?"

"All the way up my inner thighs."

"I thought you weren't in the mood to fool
around."

"I changed my mind."

Her eyes hot and glittering, she raised her
hips and tugged on her pajama bottoms. Liam
pulled them off, along with her panties. He took
his time getting to where she wanted him, caressing and teasing and slowly moving toward
her center. Restless, she opened her thighs and
bared herself.

So beautiful. Wet. Totally turned on, he fingered her, savoring her quick intake of breath and her flushed skin. He kept up the attention until she was writhing and moaning. Almost there. "Let go, Gracie."

He touched her in the right place at the right speed and she orgasmed. Watching her let go, he almost embarrassed himself. When she went still, he leaned in and kissed her lips. "All better?"

Calm and relaxed, she gave a drowsy smile. "Much."

"Then my work here is done." He pulled her robe over her bare legs, then stood. "Time for me to head home."

She stared at his straining zipper. "Are you sure?"

For now, helping her was enough. "I'm good. I'll let myself out. See you at the studio in the morning."

Standing outside her door, he adjusted himself. The wait for the elevator wasn't long. Despite his painful hard-on, he felt good that he'd given Grace pleasure without jeopardizing the progress he'd made since she'd walked away from him.

He'd meant what he'd told his crewmates— he had no interest in setting himself up for fresh heartbreak with her. This new relationship between them was purely physical, and he intended to enjoy it while it lasted.

He exited at the lobby, hunched his shoulders against the frigid cold, and strode into the night.

~

RESTED after a good night's sleep, Grace hummed as she showered and dressed. She was awful glad Liam had come over last night. He'd taken her mind off her troubles and given her the physical release she so badly needed. They weren't getting back together and they weren't seeing each other in the normal sense, but the physical side of their relationship was as powerful as ever.

She wanted more and could have it—as long as she kept her secrets and her love locked inside.

Which she'd managed to do for almost a year and a half. True, during that time she hadn't seen Liam, let alone savored the feel of his arms around her or the heat of his touch. The physical act of his kisses and loving made her feel alive for the first time in what seemed like forever.

If only she were free to let her true feelings out... But the thought of telling Liam the truth after such a long time and the fallout that would follow was too horrible to contemplate. He was all about openness and honesty, and since Robert's death, she'd been neither. For good reasons—her shame and the pact of silence she and her mother had made.

If she were to tell Liam, she knew exactly what would happen, had seen the fallout when someone he cared about abused his trust. He'd talked about the brief affair his mother had had with the family friend he'd once called Uncle Joe, right before she died. Even after ten years, his eyes grew icy and hard at the mention of Joe, who'd apologized, but Liam refused to forgive.

Which was understandable, but to bear the brunt of that loathing... Anything was better than that. Her only choice was to draw the line at physical. Or walk away again. Which for some irrational reason, she didn't want to do.

On the drive to the studio, she went a few blocks out of the way and stopped at Rosemary's to pick up two strong coffees and several freshly baked poppy seed muffins.

Five minutes after she turned up the heat in the studio, Liam pulled up in front. No motorcycle today—way too cold. Her heart lifted and certain body parts tingled. She let him in. There was something about a gorgeous man carrying tools...

"Look at you with your toolbox," she murmured as she relocked the door behind him.

"Like this, do you? I'll have to remember that."

His gaze roved over her with undisguised lust. He pulled her into a long kiss that made up for having to get up so early. She was sinking against him when he let her go. "I can't fix your wiring problems, but I can recommend an expert for later. Meanwhile, I'm going to set you up with ELT-approved surge protectors. ELT stands for 'Electrical Testing Laboratories.' " He sniffed the air. "I smell coffee and something from the bakery."

"You always did have a good nose. On the way here I stopped at Rosemary's. Feeding and caffeinating you is the least I can do."

"Then I lucked out this morning. You look rested."

She was. "For the first time in a long time, I slept through the night. Thanks to you. I owe you."

"I'll hold you to that."

His slate gray eyes turned molten silver. The tingling inside Grace became a needy ache. She wanted to jump his bones. Would have, if her first appointment had been scheduled for an hour later. She checked her watch. "I have a ton to do before my nine-thirty comes in."

"Right." Suddenly all business, Liam stuffed half a muffin in his mouth, then grabbed his tools. "After you show me the office circuit breaker, I'll replace those surge protectors."

Twenty minutes later, he'd jotted notes for the updated wiring she needed, supplied her with the name and number of a guy he recommended, and replaced her four aging surge protectors with two new ones.

"Until you get that wiring checked and updated, you're going to have to make do with what you have," he said.

When he pulled her into her office in the back, she didn't resist. They shared a steamy kiss that flared into more, along with serious groping and moaning. When he released her, she was sizzling.

"Thanks for the coffee and muffin," he said. "Enjoy your day."

She stayed in her office until the door clicked shut behind him.

6

S aturday night, Liam met Tony and Nate at a sports bar on the west side of town. Both men had given him a hand gutting the Laundromat, and the beer and food was on him. Rafe had helped too, but Jillian had dragged him to a chick flick she wanted to see.

"Summer's out Christmas shopping tonight with her sister and some of their friends," Tony said over a pitcher and nachos. "She ordered me to go out too. She says I'm driving her crazy, hovering around. But hey, her due date is in three weeks. She could deliver at any time."

"You keep your cell phone turned on, right?" Liam asked. "Whether or not you're with her when her time comes, you'll know."

"That's exactly what Rafe said." Tony snorted. "I'll remind him of that in seven months."

Liam imagined himself hovering like Tony if Grace was expecting, then frowned. The days of planning a future together were behind them.

"When are you seeing Grace again?" Tony asked.

"No idea."

"But you're planning to see her soon, right?"

Nate's cell phone pinged with a message, saving Liam from another conversation about him and Grace. The whole crew knew they were involved on a physical level, and wanted updates. As if.

Nate checked the screen and grinned. "Becca's home from work. She wants me at her place, stat."

Moments later, Tony also received a text. "Summer's leaving the mall now. Gotta go."

Liam envied them. "I should leave too," he said. "I'm having breakfast with my grandpa in the morning and I need to swing by the grocery before it closes."

He paid the bill and parted ways with his crewmates.

In the car, he thought about texting Grace and suggesting they get together tonight. Trouble was, he really needed to pick up a few things for his grandpa. Never mind—in the morning he'd text her and ask if she wanted to hang out in the afternoon.

A Sunday afternoon with Grace, fooling around like old times... The thought had him all hot and bothered in a very noticeable way. He distracted himself by making a mental list of what to buy. That worked, and by the time he headed into the grocery, his body was behaving itself.

MARGUERITE HAD INVITED Grace to come with her to Orchard High for the annual holiday concert, where Marguerite's sixteen-year-old cousin Julie was playing a violin solo. Grace drove, and when the concert ended she congratulated the girl and chatted with the rest of the family. Then she and Marguerite left.

"I meant what I told Julie," Grace said in the car. "I enjoyed listening to her play. She's talented."

Marguerite beamed. "When she graduates, she plans to attend Juilliard and become a professional musician. If she gets in. Her violin teacher thinks she has a good chance."

"Wouldn't that be something."

"It's early yet," Marguerite said. "Do you have time to get a drink and catch up?"

"Can we do that after Christmas? The candy dish in the front office is almost empty and I'm out of refills. Plus I need to replenish my stash at home. I won't have time to go to the store in the morning—too much to do—and I want to get it done before the store closes tonight. Let's fill each other in on the drive to your house. You haven't mentioned the cute guy you helped at the

Cheesery last week—the one with the romantic hero name."

"Zane. He's who I wanted to talk about. He came back the other day. Apparently everyone at his sister's party raved about the combo of the cheese with the fruit sauce. He wanted to sample some of the other cheeses we talked about, but I really think he came in to see me." Marguerite grinned. "We flirted a lot. He has the most beautiful eyes and the sexiest smile."

"You mentioned his eyes last time, but not the smile. That smile sounds dangerous." Grace understood. More than once, Liam's smile had turned her insides into a quivering mass of want.

"He spent a fair amount on cheese, and I found out what he does for a living. Something called design technology that has to do with machinery and obsolescence risk, whatever that is. He sent all kinds of 'I'm interested' signals, so I invited him to coffee."

"Good for you! When are you meeting?"

"With the Christmas season in full swing, I can't take a lot of time off, but I do happen to be free tomorrow morning. We have a date at the Coffee Shack."

"I may not read as many romance novels as you, but I so enjoy a good love story. This has the beginnings of one."

"I'll find out. Speaking of romance, what's the latest with Liam?"

"I saw him Thursday when he stopped by the studio and helped with a wiring issue."

"I'll bet he did." Sly smile.

"It's the truth." Grace thought about the kisses and touching that had followed. "And all right, before he left we made out, but not for as long as I wanted. Along with you and everyone else in retail and the photography business, I'm too busy."

"Never for serious smooching. You're getting back together—I know it."

"No, but I *have* been fantasizing about having sex with him." A lot.

"And you say you're not involved. Ha!"

"I never said that. We're involved, but only physically."

Even in the dark, Grace could see her friend's speculative look. "We lost our virginity within a month of each other," Marguerite reminded her.

Grace nodded. "You and Matt, me with Hal. We compared notes. They'd have died if they'd known." They both laughed.

"Then later, you were there to hold my hand when Matt and I broke up," Marguerite said. "I did the same for you when Hal moved on. We've supported each other through all our past relationships and every breakup."

"And your point is?"

"In all that time, you've never slept with a man you didn't have strong feelings for."

Her friend had no idea. "Don't get me wrong

—I care about Liam and I know he cares about me. But this isn't serious, and we don't have to get back together to want each other physically." Even saying the words made Grace twitchy. "That connection between us has always been strong, and still is."

"Ah, now I understand. You're like Jennika and Dennis." Jennika was Marguerite's older sister, and Dennis was her ex. "They've been sleeping together since their divorce. She says they're great in bed, but that they positively, absolutely will never get back together. Seems to work for them."

"Exactly. Chemistry."

"Let me get this straight. You want Liam physically, but you're sure you don't want to get back with him. Not even a little bit?"

What Grace really wanted didn't matter. The loving relationship she and Liam had once shared was no longer possible, so why waste time on wishful thinking? She braked to a halt at a four-way stop. "No, and he doesn't want to get back with me either."

Marguerite gave her a long look. "Why do I get the feeling you're not being straight with me?"

Because Grace wasn't. For a moment she was tempted to confide in her friend, but that would be like opening a Pandora's box of questions she didn't want to answer or explain. Besides, she and her mom had made the pact not to tell anyone.

"Come on, Grace, we've been besties since middle school. We tell each other everything."

"It's a tangled mess and I don't want to get into the details." That was the most she dared to say.

"Well, shoot. I guess we don't share everything."

Grace could tell Marguerite was hurt. "Don't be offended," she pleaded. "Please, understand that I can't talk about it." Ever.

"All right, but if you need to, I'm here."

"I know, and I love you for that." Grace pulled up in front of her friend's building. "Thanks for inviting me tonight."

"Thanks for driving."

After a quick hug, her friend hopped out of the car.

Grace checked her watch. The grocery would close soon, but she had time to run in and get the candy.

There were only a few shoppers inside. After grabbing a hand basket, she stopped at a candy cane display and added a bag to the basket. Then she hurried through the bakery section to see what they had—a treat for tonight or breakfast in the morning—but that area was pretty much cleaned out. Next, she visited the candy aisle, where she found several bags of foil-wrapped holiday chocolates. The cookie section the next aisle over called to her. Better check that out. She turned into the aisle and spotted Liam.

Her heart sighed and her entire body perked up. She headed straight for him.

7

Liam added a package of fig bars, his grandpa's favorite, to his half-filled cart. Some sixth sense made him glance up. Grace was moving his way, clutching a shopping basket. Her winter coat was unbuttoned, revealing dressy pants and a red velvet top. Date clothes. Who had she been out with, he wondered, gripping the cart handle so tight, a blister on his palm burned.

She gave him a wary look and he realized he was scowling. He had no right to feel possessive. Forcing a bland expression, he nodded. "Hey. I didn't expect to run into you here on a Saturday night."

"Because I live such an exciting life?"

"You and me both." He glanced at her basket. "Late-night candy run, huh?"

Her lips quirked. "You caught me. Most of these are for the bowl for my clients at the studio, but a girl has to have her chocolate."

"You do, that's for sure. I know you didn't dress up to buy sweets."

"Hardly." She laughed. "Marguerite and I went to a concert at Orchard High. Her cousin played an awesome violin solo. What a talent."

No date, then. Liam relaxed. "That's a nice school. I played a couple of away football games there."

"You still look like a linebacker."

Her gaze trailed over him, and stopped for a moment at his crotch. It started to react all over again. Damn, he wanted her.

"What are you doing here?" she asked.

"Picking up a few things for my grandpa. We're having breakfast in the morning."

"That's nice. Tell him I said hello, unless the mention of my name causes an awkward conversation."

"Why would it?"

"Because we're not together anymore."

No, and Liam meant to keep it that way. "He likes you—he'll be cool."

The background Christmas music paused for an announcement. "Our store is closing in ten minutes."

"I'd better hustle." Grace added several packages of cookies to her basket.

He fell into step with her, and they headed for the empty checkout area. In no time, they paid. He'd wanted to be with her in the worst way tonight, and here she was. For sure, he wasn't

ready to say good-bye. "Do you want to go someplace and get something to eat?" he asked on the
way out.

"I wouldn't mind dessert. Where are you
thinking?"

"Marv's has great pies. So does The Rogue.
Your choice."

"As much as I like Marv's, it gets noisy on a
Saturday night."

"The Rogue it is. I'll drive, then drop you back
here. While you load your groceries into your car,
I'll pull around and pick you up."

RIDING shotgun in Liam's Yukon was like old
times. "This isn't a date, okay?" Grace said, to
make sure he didn't get the wrong idea.

"The thought never entered my mind." He
angled her a look she couldn't read. "We're not
seeing each other and not dating. On that we
agree. We didn't plan this—we ran into each
other and decided to grab something to eat. No
big deal."

Relieved, she nodded.

The Rogue was crowded, mostly with groups
of teens texting, laughing, and acting silly like the
kids they were. Grace and Liam found a table
near the back of the restaurant.

"This is almost as noisy as Marv's, only
without the super loud music," she said.

"We didn't think about the kids."

A high school girl with hair the color of red Kool-Aid arrived to take their orders. She gave Liam a bright smile. "Hey, you're Mr. December. My mom has the calendar on our kitchen wall."

Liam flashed his teeth. "That's great. Tell us about your pies tonight."

"Cherry, chocolate silk, coconut cream, and pecan," she rattled off.

Grace's mouth watered. "Chocolate silk with whipped cream, and a cup of herbal tea."

The girl jotted the selection on her order pad and turned to Liam.

"Double cheeseburger with the works, and curly fries. For dessert, black coffee and cherry pie, heated, with two scoops of vanilla ice cream."

As the waitress left, Grace raised her eyebrows at Liam. "Late dinner, or is this a snack?"

"A little of both. I ate something with Tony and Nate at a sports bar awhile ago."

"Let me guess—the nachos special, loaded with everything."

He shrugged. He'd always had a big appetite —for food and sex. Some nights, they'd hardly slept for all the lovemaking... She shifted in her seat and folded her hands on the table. "I haven't seen Nate or Tony in ages. How are they?"

"The big news is that Tony's girlfriend Summer is due to have a baby in a few weeks. They aren't saying whether it's a boy or a girl, and we're taking bets on that at the station."

"What's your best guess?" she asked.

"Girl. And Nate is dating Becca Chambers. You might know her—she owns Second Hand Rose. I told you Rafe and Jillian got married but I didn't mention that she's pregnant too."

Grace felt a pang of longing. It hadn't been that long ago that she and Liam had discussed having children someday. Not a chance of that now. She forced a smile. "Two babies. Pretty exciting."

"Yeah." Liam seemed on the verge of commenting, but didn't.

"You're right, I know Becca from Second Hand Rose. But I've never met Summer." At one time, Grace had been friendly with several of Liam's crewmates' girlfriends—Sam, Jillian, Wanda, and Hallie—but not so much anymore. Most had reached out to her after Robert's death, but she'd felt so bad about hurting Liam that she hadn't wanted to face them. Yet more repercussions from her father's dirty tricks. "Will they be at the party at Auntie's Place?"

He shook his head. "Firefighters only, plus you and Auntie's Place staff members. And the kids and their families."

"Oh, my gosh—I just realized the party is in less than two weeks. I haven't bought my Secret Santa presents for those boys."

"I haven't bought mine either."

Liam's meal arrived. "Help yourself to the

fries and tell me about your photo shoots today," he said while he ate.

Eager to share something light and happy, Grace launched into the details. "This was a fun day. It started with six widows ages seventy through eighty-four. They showed up dressed as elves in short green dresses, striped red tights, elf shoes that curled up at the toes, and green Santa hats. Constance, who's in her early seventies and the 'head elf,' could win a contest for a Mrs. Claus lookalike. Short, round, with white hair and twinkling eyes."

"I can picture it now."

Remembering, Grace smiled. "You have no idea. They were a total hoot—making the silliest puns, cracking jokes, and having a ball. I promised to send their proofs tomorrow. They gave me permission to add a copy of the photo they choose to my portfolio."

"Like the books that your father put together for people to look through," Liam said as the desserts arrived.

He would mention *him*. It put a bad taste in Grace's mouth, which she drowned out with a bite of pie. "They left laughing. I couldn't help but compare them to my mother. She's not even sixty yet, but sometimes she seems older than the woman who's eighty-four." *Thanks again, Robert.* Grace ate more pie. "I want her to find her zest for life again."

"She will. So will you."

Would she?

Liam leaned toward her. "Give yourself time. It'll happen."

He caught her hands in his warm, firm grasp. Immediately she felt better. If only she could crawl onto his lap like the other night and let physical hunger drown out her problems. For that, they needed privacy.

She reclaimed her hands. "After the elves left, I photographed two dads and their baby, then a Realtor. Rosemary was my last shoot of the day."

"Our Rosemary, from Rosemary's Breakfast Nook?"

"One and the same." Grace had enjoyed many a breakfast there, both with friends and with Liam and his crewmates. "José was with her." The restaurant owner and her cook were dating. "Like everyone else, they're in a big hurry to get the proofs, select their photo, and mail their holiday cards. Which means I'll be spending tomorrow getting the proofs ready and sending them to everyone I saw today."

"You really aren't taking any time off."

"Except for tonight."

"It paid off. You seem relaxed."

"I had no idea how badly I needed an evening away from the job."

Grace was having a good time. She didn't want the evening to end, but The Rogue was about to close.

"That's two places we've been kicked out of." Flirting with a smile, Liam signaled for the bill.

"You make us sound crazy wild."

"Depends on your definition of 'crazy wild.' Care to discuss that at my place?"

Suddenly dead serious, he studied her. Under that intent gaze, her body thrilled. "I'm not at all tired, and I do keep thinking about how beautiful that octagonal room must be at night with the fire going."

"You don't want to miss out on that. Back to 'crazy wild'..."

His hot eyes promised other things she wouldn't want to miss. In full agreement, she nodded. He rose and pulled her to her feet. "Let's go."

8

I n the powder room off Liam's kitchen, Grace popped a mint into her mouth. Both to freshen her breath and to think for a minute while he started the fire upstairs.

As badly as she wanted to be with Liam, and she wanted that more than anything, she was nervous. With her feelings for him as strong as ever, she wasn't sure she could hide them. She considered telling him she'd changed her mind and didn't want to stay.

As she exited the powder room, he was waiting for her. "The fire's going and—" With a frown, he cut himself off. "What's running through that brain of yours?"

"Are we going to have sex?" she asked, unable to control her anxious tone.

"Not unless you want to. Hell, we don't have to do anything. If you'd rather leave after you see the room, I'll take you straight back to your car."

With that reassurance, Grace realized that

any pressure she felt came from inside her. "Show it to me and we'll play the rest by ear?"

"Fine by me. You'll be in charge."

"I like that. By the way, are you clean?"

"Yes. What about you? Still on the pill?"

She nodded.

"Come on." Taking her hand, he climbed the stairs with her.

The octagonal room was dark, with only fire-light to guide them. Reflections of the cheerful gas flame danced on the windows opposite. Soft jazz played in the background.

"You weren't kidding—at night this room is special in a totally different way than in daylight." She noted the thick quilt and two throw pillows near the fireplace. "You put that there for us."

"Yeah. Ignore it."

"I wouldn't mind sitting there and watching the fire."

"Make yourself comfortable."

After removing her shoes, she sat down and crossed her legs. Liam joined her. He wasn't close enough to touch her, but she was intensely aware of him.

"The fire is mesmerizing," she said. "I could watch it for hours."

"A wood fire is better, but this is a close second."

Staring at the fire in the cozy room beside Liam felt romantic and intimate. Grace craved his touch. She snuck a look at him, but he was transfixed by the fire. He'd meant what he'd said—she was in charge.

She scooted closer. He cocked an eyebrow. "You were too far away," she explained.

"What do you want me to do?"

"Touch me."

"Like this?" He put his arm around her shoulders.

"It's a start." With her palm on his massive thigh, she leaned up and kissed the underside of his chin. "Come down here so I can reach your lips."

"You're bossing me around and it's hot," he said.

"I've never heard that one before, but I'll take it. Lower your head and let me kiss—"

The next she knew, she was on his lap, engaged in a deep, wet kiss she never wanted to end.

Far too soon it did. "Satisfied?" he asked, anchoring her against his erection.

"Not quite," she teased. "I—"

He palmed her breasts and brushed his thumbs over her nipples. Whatever she'd been about to say faded from her mind. Her top disappeared. He'd taken charge, after all. She didn't mind.

His hands, oh, his hands. Loving her breasts, making her wet between her legs. His mouth on her nipples through her bra.

"I think we're getting to the meat of 'crazy wild,' " she breathed.

"We barely started." He went back to business.

"Wait." Pushing him away, she removed her bra, then cupped and lifted her breasts. "For you."

More licking and tasting, driving her into a frenzy of need.

"Easy," he said around her nipple. "Every time you wiggle like that, I get closer to the point of no return."

"Like this?" She did it again.

"You minx. You're in trouble now." He reached for the button on her pants.

With a moan, she raised her hips. "Make love with me, and for God's sake, hurry."

He set her off his lap. "On your back. Now."

He stripped off the rest of her clothes, then his own. The firelight glinted off his beautiful body, burnishing every honed muscle and scar earned from years of firefighting. He kissed her until she was breathless, kissed his way down her stomach. By the time he crawled between her legs, she was dying for him.

"I believe this is where we left off the other night," he said. On his knees, he parted her folds.

She lay back, her head on the pillow. He remembered what she liked, each lick and touch bringing her closer to release, but not quite taking her where she longed to go. Reduced to begging, she groaned. "Liam, please let me come."

He gave her a wicked grin. "I've been waiting for you to tell me."

He did something amazing with his tongue and fingers. She shattered, riding a wave of bliss that seemed to last a long time. As the pleasure began to fade, he entered her. Deep and still. She was utterly sated, and not sure she could climax a second time. But he reached between them and brought her to the brink again. As she shuddered and let go, so did he.

When it ended, he rolled beside her and placed his hand on her hip. "I'd call that crazy wild."

"Mind-blowing crazy wild," she corrected. Smiling in the afterglow of loving him, she started to snuggle closer.

Then she remembered—they didn't belong to each other, not anymore. Even if her aching heart told her otherwise.

Biting back a howl at the unfairness of life, she started to untangle herself from his grasp.

He levered himself up on his arm and frowned. "Hey, are you okay?"

No. After their enjoyable evening and romantic, out-of-this-world sex, hiding her true emotions was almost unbearable.

"Gracie?"

"I'm fine," she lied. "I need a towel."

"Relax—I'll get you one."

He rose and padded from the room, taking

his glorious self away from her. Already she missed him.

She'd known better than to get involved with him again, yet she'd plunged right back into the relationship with kisses and aching desire. Tonight, she'd recklessly welcomed him into her body and her heart.

As wonderful as making love with him was, it'd been a giant mistake that made everything worse.

IN THE BATHROOM, Liam cleaned himself up and shook his head. As usual, sex with Grace had shot him into the stratosphere. He'd felt fantastic, right up until he tugged her close to his side when they finished.

She'd always liked to cuddle afterward. Not anymore. For her, tonight truly had been about sex, period.

He'd wanted that too—or believed he did. Buried inside her, the two of them joined as deeply and intimately as a man and woman could be, that changed, his brain taking a backseat to his feelings. For a few mindless seconds after they'd collapsed in contentment, he'd felt bonded to her. Whole, grounded.

Then she'd broken away, breaking the illusion. For her, the strong connection between them no longer existed, and by default he'd lost it too.

He missed it, mourned it, and was still clueless why the relationship had soured for her. Grief and juggling photography with learning how to run the studio were only part of the reason. She refused to tell him the rest. Fool that he was, he'd let that go and hung around when any man with half a brain would've steered clear.

Trouble was, around Grace his smarts disappeared. As always, he'd fallen under her spell and lost himself in her softness and passion. Bad move. Tonight he'd crossed his own line, the one he'd drawn to protect himself so that he could move on.

He wanted her back.

Not happening, buddy. She didn't want a true partnership with him. Never had, and wasn't going to change. With her, it was either physical or nothing. And physical wasn't enough.

Best get her out of here ASAP and pull himself together. Play the "We're better off as friends" card. The kind who didn't see much of each other.

Back in the room, he found her sitting up with the quilt wrapped around her and the firelight flickering across her face. After handing her the wash cloth, he collected her clothes from the rug.

"Thanks."

Keeping the quilt in place with one hand, she

stood and held out the other for her things. No smile, no eye contact. *Right there with you, Grace.* "Having second thoughts?" he said.

"Yeah."

"Me too. We were in an awful big rush to have sex."

"I agree." She bit her lip. "I don't think we should do it again."

Good to know they were on the same wavelength. He nodded.

"I'll dress in the spare bedroom," she said.

After flipping on the lights, he stepped into his clothes and shut the fire off. Once he returned the pillows to the couch the room looked as if he and Grace had never made love here. If only banishing her from his head and heart were that easy.

She returned and set the folded quilt on the couch. "I'm ready."

"I'll take you to your car."

"Where do we go from here?" she said as he sped through the darkness.

"We dial back, be casual friends—if we run into each other we say hello, then go our separate ways."

"That'll work."

The road was mostly deserted, and in no time he pulled into the grocery parking lot and braked beside her minivan, the lone vehicle. "Good luck with those proofs."

"Thanks. Have fun with your grandpa."

"I always do." Reaching across the seat, he opened her door and let her out.

9

At eighty, Liam's grandpa, after whom he was named, was still tall and hearty, with twinkling gray eyes behind a pair of bifocals, and a full head of silvery hair. Liam set down the groceries and manbraced his only living blood relative. "Hey, Grandpa."

"It's good to see you. Hungry?"

"You know it. Need a hand with breakfast?"

"Sure, after I pour myself another coffee. You look like you could use a cup."

Liam had already taken a mug from the cabinet. "Late night."

After he gulped a few hefty sips, his grandpa eyed him. "Better now?'

"Much."

"I'll scramble the eggs, you make the toast."

"Deal. Tony, Nate, and Rafe helped me strip the old drywall off that Laundromat I bought," Liam said while they cooked. He liked to keep his grandfather informed. "If things go as planned, the place will be rewired by the end of next week."

"That's great. Then what?"

"New plumbing. It'll be good to have both done before Christmas."

When the food was ready, they sat down. "Tell me about your new flavor of the month," Grandpa said over the meal.

Liam scoffed. "You make me sound like a player. I'm not that bad."

"You said you had a late night."

Not about to discuss that, Liam shoveled a forkful of eggs into his mouth.

"If I were young and single, I'd be doing what you're doing. I did, till your grandma came along."

Liam's grandmother had died ten years ago, after fifty years of marriage. His grandfather had been on his own since.

"You were a lucky man, Grandpa."

"Don't I know it. She was the best thing that ever happened to me. Got your Christmas shopping done?"

"Haven't even started. I'll do it next week. You haven't said what you want this year."

"If my doctor hadn't ordered me to give up my pipe, I'd ask for a couple of tins of Captain Earle's pipe tobacco. You could sneak me some anyway."

"No dice, but I will spring for a pack of spearmint gum," Liam deadpanned.

"Very funny." Grandpa leaned his forearms on

the table. "What I really want is to see you married and happy."

He would bring that up. Liam thought about Grace and frowned. "Not this year."

"You sound grumpy. Your date last night must've gone badly."

"I never kiss and tell, so quit fishing for info. By the way, I ran into Grace. She says hi."

"Tell her hello back. Of all your girlfriends, she was my favorite. You were with her longer than most."

"I liked her too, but thinking about her is a waste of time. I'm moving on."

"You said that months ago."

Liam shrugged. "I've been dating."

Or had been until he'd started up with Grace again. As of now he was back in the game. Might even take the redhead from the costume rental place out. Too bad he'd tossed her card. What was her name?

The old man's eyes narrowed. "I know that look. You still care about her."

No point denying the truth. "I always will, but nothing will come of it. Grace made it clear that she doesn't want to get involved again. I don't want that either. We're barely friends."

Yeah, right. And Guff's Lake was filled with buried treasure. Should've skipped the trip to the grocery last night. He wouldn't have run into her and would've been in a better place this morning. Licking his wounds all over again sucked.

And his grandfather knew it. "Hogwash. Get her back."

"I told you, she's not interested."

"You know good and well that once we Gibson men fall in love, it's for good. Me, your dad—"

"Look where that got him. He wanted Mom back even after she left us to run off with Joe."

"Don't forget, she was headed back to you and your dad when she got in that car accident. He loved her so much, he was going to take her back with open arms. Forgiveness is a big part of love. Grace is the right woman for you. The *only* one."

Liam snorted. "I disagree."

"Then you're a fool. You tried settling for the wrong female after your parents died. That was such a bad match, it only lasted half a year. Don't make that same mistake again."

"I was twenty years old, still a kid, feeling orphaned and lost. I didn't know what I was doing. I'm older and smarter now. I made a big mistake when Grace and I first got together—I rushed into the relationship when I knew better." He added "glutton for punishment" to the long list of derogatory names he reserved for himself for repeating the same thing with the same woman. "I'll meet the right woman—she's out there."

"You always have been a stubborn jackass," his grandfather muttered. "Prove me wrong, then, and find her. You need a partner to share your life with."

"There's something we agree on. It may take awhile, but it will happen."

"Don't take too long. I'd like to cash in my chips knowing you're settled."

Liam rolled his eyes. "You'll be around another twenty years."

"God willing."

SUNDAY AFTERNOON, Grace's mom called and invited her over for an impromptu dinner. "It's my day off, and I felt like cooking," she said. "I'm making biscuits and that beef stew you like. Come over and share it with me."

Grace's mouth watered. "Perfect timing—I'm just finishing work for the day. What can I bring?"

"A bottle of red wine and yourself."

Another call came in. Marguerite, no doubt to tell her about this morning's coffee date with Zane. Grace wanted to hear about that and also needed to talk about Liam.

"I should take that, Mom. I'll be over soon." She disconnected from her mom and answered Marguerite's call. "Hey, you. How was coffee?"

"We had a great time. He didn't ask me out, but I think he will."

"I'll cross my fingers. You'll never guess what I did after I dropped you off." Grace told her about running into Liam and what had happened. "I feel pretty bad about it. I don't mean the sex. It was amazing. But the emotional part..." She couldn't get into that without sharing her secrets. "What I mean is, I shouldn't have slept with him. He also had second thoughts. We agreed it won't happen again."

"I'm not surprised. Didn't I tell you? You're not a woman who can keep sex and your heart separate."

"I wish I'd listened. Too late now. I should go —Mom invited me over for dinner and I need to get a bottle of wine. Thanks for the update on Zane."

"Hopefully, I'll have more soon. Say hi to your mom."

Sometime later, Grace walked into the kitchen she'd known forever to find her mom humming as she added seasonings to the stew pot.

"That smells delicious," she said and kissed her mother's cheek. "You're in a good mood."

"I am. I made a new friend, a woman I met working those two extra shifts at the hardware store. Her name is Mona. She's divorced and manages one of the food banks. She was hired for the holiday season too. She has a son and a daughter, both in their early twenties. We went out after work last night and had the best time, like we've known each other forever."

Grace hadn't seen her eyes sparkle in ages. She smiled. "That's great, Mom."

"It was a relief not to think about your father. What did you do last night?"

"Marguerite's cousin Julie played a concert at Orchard High. We went together." Grace shared the details. She skipped over seeing Liam.

"That sounds fun. You and Marguerite haven't spent an evening together in too long."

"Because we're both super busy, especially during the holiday season."

"Have you seen Liam since the last time we talked?" her mother asked.

Trust her to bring up the subject Grace most wanted to avoid. "I don't really want to talk about him, Mom. It hurts too much."

"I understand, honey, and I'm sorry."

"So am I."

10

For days on end, Grace worked continuously, often spending ten or more hours at the studio. Photo shoots, fine tuning images, and the back and forth emails and phone calls with each client... Rinse and repeat, nonstop. Which was normal in the weeks leading up to Christmas, but now made her feel like a hamster running on a wheel.

Most clients were easily satisfied. A few insisted on retakes or discounts, demands that took additional time and cut into any chance of sitting down to a decent meal or relaxing. At least when she worked, she wasn't brooding about Liam.

She did that when she fell into bed at night. Miserable and also relieved that she hadn't heard from him. She hadn't reached out to him either —they needed to focus on their own lives.

In the morning she always felt better, ready to face another hectic day. But by Thursday evening, sick to death of working, brooding, and sleeping, she hit a wall. If she didn't do something different right now, she would surely lose her mind.

The holiday party at Auntie's Place was one week away and she still hadn't bought the secret Santa gifts. The two brothers' wish lists included brand-name sports clothing and equipment. Getting to the mall on the outskirts of town meant a long drive, but with tons of stores, doing so seemed well worth the trip. While she was at it, she'd do the rest of her shopping there.

She made herself a sandwich, grabbed a handful of chocolate marshmallow Santas to eat on the way, and headed out. Thanks to rush hour traffic, vehicles clogged the highway, the line of headlights bright as far as she could see.

By the time she arrived, the mall's four-level garage was full. Lighted signs directed her to another parking area a few blocks away. Bundled up against the weather, she didn't mind the walk back to the mall. Between the exercise and the brisk cold, work and her troubles seemed far away. For the first time in a while, she felt good.

How long had it been since she'd simply enjoyed the great outdoors?

Snow flurries sprinkled the air, twinkling in the streetlights along the way. So pretty. By the time she reached the mall entrance, her eyes were watering from the cold, and snow dusted her coat and scarf. Grace brushed off her sleeves and stepped inside—into a madhouse. People everywhere, talking and moving one way or the other, the sounds competing with the background Christmas music.

After checking her coat and scarf—no point lugging them around while shopping—Grace studied the "You are here" mall map. The store she wanted was some distance down. She made her way through the throng, noting the long lines of shoppers snaking out the doors of many shops.

The sports store was packed. As unsmiling people jostled past, her good mood faded and she questioned the wisdom of coming here at night. Too late now. Setting her jaw, she fought her way toward the clothing area. Besides several rounders and racks, there were multiple shelves with still more clothes.

Well, shoot. With so many options, how was she supposed to choose? She decided to look at the sports equipment. That meant another trek through the hordes to the rear of the store. And another wide selection.

Feeling way out of her element, she searched for a clerk to advise her, but even they had lines of waiting shoppers, many impatient and unfriendly. Grace was rapidly getting there too.

Enough already. Executing an about-face, she left the store empty-handed. What she needed was a place to sit and collect herself. Naturally, every available bench and chair was taken. Determined to find something, she searched the area. No seats, but she did spot Liam.

In faded jeans and a flannel shirt rolled up at the cuffs, he looked gorgeous. But then, he always did. Such a ruggedly handsome man. Her rebel heart did a happy dance, which she ignored. They'd agreed to be casual friends, and she intended to behave that way. Pretending she wasn't swooning, she curled her lips and waved.

His responding smile was as phony as hers. "And we run into each other yet again. How are you?"

"A little too busy, but otherwise I'm okay. You?"

"Doing well."

A group of women with serious expressions and bulging shopping bags passed by. Grace followed them with her eyes. "Do they know something I don't? Maybe special Christmas sales at certain stores? Whatever the reason, I'm questioning my sanity for deciding to do my Christmas shopping now. Marguerite swears the best time to come to the mall during the holiday season is dinnertime, when families are at home eating." She scoffed. "Not tonight."

"I hear that. You'd think Christmas was tomorrow instead of several weeks away. We're supposed to get a big snow later tonight. My guess is, people are trying to squeeze in their shopping before then."

"Could be. When I came in, a light snow was falling."

"So I noticed." He squinted at her. "You can't

have been here long—you don't have any packages."

"I don't see you with any either. I'm supposed to shop for the two brothers from Auntie's Place. Anton is twelve. The top items on his list are a basketball and a LeBron James jersey. Jordan, age ten, wants a baseball mitt and a Chicago Cubs cap."

"That stuff should be easy to find. There's a sports store farther down the mall."

"I've already been there. I must've counted a dozen different James jerseys and Cubs caps. The same with baseball mitts and basketballs. How am I supposed to know which ones to get the boys?"

"Check with someone who works there. They'll tell you what's popular with kids those ages."

"Believe me, I tried. The clerks are swamped. I was in a decent mood when I arrived, but the other shoppers were short-tempered and pushy. Now I'm crabby and I still don't have any gifts."

"I'm not having an easy time either. I'm buying for a six-month-old boy and his four-year-old sister. The parents asked for a winter coat and pajamas for the baby. The girl wants a princess dress and a book."

Poor man looked utterly clueless. "I have a fair idea what the girl is into," Grace said. "I've been photographing kids of all ages for weeks."

Liam stroked his chin, reminding her of his

grandpa. "I know we're supposed to say hi and part ways, but we both need help. I think we should team up and get the job done. Then I can get the hell out of here."

Work together, then separate—where was the harm in that? "Okay."

"Let's start at the sports store and figure out what to get those boys."

"YOU'RE SURE a snowsuit with a smiling train on it is the right thing for a six-month-old?" Liam asked. Due to the large number of shoppers in the children's apparel store, he and Grace stood close to each other, almost touching.

Her hair was a little crazy, but cute. Out of habit, he reached out to smooth it. Then stopped himself and dropped his hand. The decision to be casual friends had transformed her. She was relaxed and more like her old self. Touching her could change that, and he wanted her mood to last until they finished shopping.

Oblivious to his thoughts, she compared two snowsuits. "The green one looks warmer. Maybe add mittens and a hat?" She tapped a finger to her lips and pointed at a display. "These look soft. Oh, look at the onesie pajamas with feet. So adorable."

"Sold." Liam added the items to the cart he'd

snagged. "Now to find a princess dress and a book."

"I'm thinking an Elsa or Anna dress from the movie *Frozen*. I noticed some when we came in." They slogged through the crowd, to a rounder filled with gauzy, kid-size gowns.

"Kinda sparkly," he said.

"Little girls love that. Either you can get her a *Frozen* book to go with, or we can stop at the bookstore and pick up one of the *Fancy Nancy* books. They're super cute."

"*Fancy Nancy?*"

Grace burst into laughter.

"What?" he said, grinning. Shopping wasn't his favorite way to spend an evening, but she made it fun. The casual friends thing was working for him too.

"You look so lost."

"About as lost as you in that sports store. I'll go with the blue dress and *Fancy Nancy*—if you don't mind a detour to the bookstore." They joined the line of people waiting to pay.

"It's on my list. I want to get a gift card for Marguerite. She likes to buy her books locally."

"Cool."

On the way to the bookstore, he spotted the department store. "Mind if we stop here first? I need to pick up my grandpa's present."

"Not at all. This is where I planned to get my mom's gift."

This store was quieter and less crowded, a

nice change. "The men's department is upstairs," Grace said. "What does your grandpa want?"

For Liam and Grace to get back together, but he wasn't going to tell her that. No sense putting a damper on their good time. "You don't want to know." He gestured to the sign for men's sleep-wear. "He could use a new bathrobe. Something warm."

"What color?"

"Navy blue."

Liam assumed he'd find something without Grace's help, but she pointed out a plush microfiber robe that seemed made for his grandfather. "What about your mom?" he asked after his purchase was bagged and in hand.

"A blouse and a pair of earrings. Women's clothing and accessories are on the main floor."

Grace chose the blouse on her own, but at the jewelry department she turned to him. "Dangling or posts?"

"Hell if I know." He pointed to a pair with deep red flowers and tiny pearls at the centers. "Those are nice."

"Pretty and classy—exactly what she'd like." Grace's smile lit him up. "You're good at this."

"A talent I didn't know I had."

Taking pity on them with the numerous bags they were both juggling by then, the cashier gave them each a jumbo-size shopping bag, along with several flat gift boxes.

"I'm all done—yay!" Grace exclaimed as they left the bookstore awhile later.

"Same, and in record time."

"You're right, we made a good team." She nodded at the gift wrap booth. "Before we leave, we may as well get everything wrapped. At least I'm going to."

"I'm all for that."

By the time the purchases were decorated in holiday paper and bows, the noise level in the mall had decreased significantly. "The crowd sure thinned out," Liam noted.

"Tomorrow's a work day and a school day, and people need to get home. Me included, after I pick up my coat. If you keep an eye on my stuff, I'll get yours too."

While he waited, he watched a man and woman about his age kid around. In a great mood, he grinned. Hanging with Grace tonight was like old times, comfortable and filled with laughter. Almost like they were a couple again.

They weren't, and he'd best remember that.

Gazing into her warm, smiling eyes when she handed him his coat, he puzzled over whether she did. Had they turned a corner of some kind tonight?

"I'm glad I ran into you, Liam," she said, adding to his confusion as they ambled toward the exit.

He wondered if maybe they had a chance together after all. But no, not possible. As much as he cared for her, he was better off forgetting her and finding someone committed to creating a true partnership that lasted, no matter what.

"I so needed to forget work for a while," she said.

"I've spent the last two days helping the electrician I hired rewire the Laundromat. Talk about a dirty job. Did I tell you what I plan to do with some of the profits I make on that place?"

She shook her head.

"I'm going to donate a percentage to the Mentoring Project I helped create to honor Gil."

She stumbled, though there was nothing in her way. "Watch your step," he said, catching hold of her arm.

"I will."

Suddenly stiff and tense, she pulled out of his grasp. Her easy warmth had vanished, along with the sweet light shining from her eyes. The wall between them was firmly back in place.

So much for her short-lived good mood. Lately, she'd become so unpredictable and touchy, he questioned whether he'd ever really known her.

Time to leave.

"I need to get going. Thanks for the shopping help." He veered away from her.

11

L iam cut toward the exit as if he couldn't get away fast enough. If Grace had had her head on straight, she'd have said no to shopping together and headed in the opposite direction. At the time, it'd seemed like a good idea.

Soon after they'd partnered up she'd slipped into the familiar pattern of delighting in his company. Walking in tandem, cracking jokes while they shopped and navigated through the holiday crowds had turned the evening from a chore to endure to an enjoyable experience. She'd forgotten about distancing herself emotionally, instead gravitating closer until her problems had faded away and she and Liam were lost in their own private world.

She'd still be floating in the bubble they'd created if he hadn't mentioned Gil. Hearing his name had popped that bubble and shoved her back into reality, where secrets and unhappiness ruled, and being herself was impossible.

Liam being Liam, he'd read her mood shift. Now, he was almost out the door.

She dragged her feet to the exit, letting him go. When the automatic door slid open and she stepped outside, she saw the decorative bushes along the entrance shrouded in white as snow fell in a thick blanket.

She could barely see a foot in front of her, although she had no trouble making out the big man facing the door. Liam seemed to be watching for her. In this weather, a big relief.

"Can you believe this?" she muttered.

"It's a real blizzard, coming down fast and furious. Where are you parked?"

"Not far—a few blocks away."

"I'm in the garage. I'll drive you to your car."

Better to keep her distance. "I don't mind walking."

"Wearing those leather ankle boots?"

He had a point. "All right."

Anyone with eyes could see that driving was risky at best. Thanks to the deepening snow and poor visibility, what should have been a three-minute drive took fifteen.

"I've never seen a snowstorm like this," she said.

"It's not what we're used to, that's for sure. Good thing I have four-wheel drive and snow tires."

Grace didn't have either. "I'm parked in the second row, over there." She frowned. "Is that the minivan? Look at the snow on the roof and windows. It's halfway up the hubcaps."

"Four or five inches and counting. Digging you out shouldn't be difficult. Did you ever get those tire chains?"

When they were together, he'd suggested she carry a set for safety purposes. First she'd been too busy to order them. Then too broke. She shook her head.

"You're not driving without them. I'll take you home."

"I'm out of your way."

"You have to get there somehow, and I don't see anyone else offering."

"What about my minivan?"

"Pick it up when the streets are plowed."

Liam pulled onto the road at a snail's pace. The heat blasting full bore, the constant tick of the windshield wipers, and the cranked-up radio volume masked his silence but not his cool detachment.

He'd shut her out. A stinging slap across the face would've hurt less. Feeling doubly bad for treating him the same way, she lowered the volume of the radio. "You're mad at me," she said, knowing she deserved his anger and more.

"Look, I'm driving under extremely hazardous conditions. If you want to get home in one piece tonight, let me focus on getting you there."

Grace shut her mouth. And wished they could be together.

Tears gathered behind her eyes. Refusing to cry in front of him, she blinked them back. The best thing to do was keep an eye on the road and adjust the heat or change the radio station when he asked.

Liam drove slowly and expertly, passing numerous abandoned vehicles along the way. Hers could easily have been one of them.

Some three hours later, he pulled up to the walkway of her building. "Thank God," she said, sighing in relief. "I don't know what I'd have done without you."

"Spent an uncomfortable night at the mall or a shelter someplace. Credit my winter tires and four-wheel drive."

"We wouldn't have made it without your skill at the wheel. It could take you another three hours to get home. You're welcome to stay here. The sofa makes into a decent bed."

"No, thanks. I wouldn't get any sleep. You wanted to talk about what happened at the mall. We were doing okay as casual friends, even having a good time—until we weren't. Without any warning or explanation you pulled away, just like after your father died. Hanging out with you is like being with a yo-yo. You're up, you're down, you're warm, you're cold. So hell, yes, I'm mad. Mostly at myself for still having feelings for you when I know better."

Grace longed to admit the same thing. More than that, to explain herself, tell him the truth and put an end to the charade she was living. She was so tired of secrets. "Liam, I—" she started, then lost her courage and went quiet.

Robert's sins were private, known only to her and her mother. She couldn't share them. Besides, she'd rather leave things as they were than destroy any last vestiges of warmth Liam felt for her.

The effort of holding herself together was almost impossible. Somehow she managed a neutral expression, even as he probed her with a questioning look.

He blew out a resigned breath and scrubbed his hand over his weary face. "When we first met, your openness was what drew me to you. I thought we were solid, a true team, partners no matter what. That disappeared. Now there's a distance between us I can't close. Maybe if I knew the cause I could do something about it. I don't, and you aren't going to tell me."

The quietly uttered words and his bleak expression carried a note of finality.

The end of any hope for a future together.

Funny, until now she hadn't realized that she still carried a tiny germ of that hope inside herself.

What a mixed-up mess she was. "I'm sorry, Liam." More than he would ever guess. "When you get home, will you text and let me know you made it?"

He nodded. The Yukon idled at the curb until she stepped inside, then pulled away and disappeared into the storm.

GRACE CRAVED the oblivion of sleep, but whirling thoughts and emotions kept her awake. Heartache, sorrow, regret, guilt, self-disgust, self-anger, rage at her father—Liam was right, her feelings seesawed all over the place. A good cry would help, but tears evaded her too.

The blizzard didn't let up until just before dawn Friday. Area meteorologists called it the worst snowstorm in a hundred years. Every one of her clients canceled due to bad road conditions. A lucky thing, as short of hiking the two miles through a foot of snow, she had no way of getting to the studio.

Anyway, she didn't feel like taking a shower or getting dressed.

Mid-afternoon, she decided to tackle one of her long list of household chores and clean out the drawers in the bathroom vanity. Getting rid of useless junk felt good. Unfortunately, the work also freed her mind to agonize and mourn what she'd lost.

Liam was gone. Really gone.

Sinking to the bathroom floor amid the trash

bags and wastebasket, Grace finally had herself a good cry. A pity party among the garbage—if that wasn't one for the books.

She was blowing her nose when her cell phone rang. She'd left it in the kitchen.

Probably a client. Pushing to her feet, she hurried to answer. "This is Grace."

"It's Constance."

The "head elf" from the group photo shoot. Grace almost smiled. "Hi."

"Do you have a cold?"

"No. My nose is a little stuffy. Some weather we're having."

"You're telling me. I've been cooped up in the house since dinner last night. What's a woman to do but bake? I made you a batch of my favorite Christmas cookies, but I couldn't get out to deliver them. So I ate them myself."

Grace's laugh surprised her and did wonders for her spirits.

"You did a terrific job on our group photo," Constance went on. "We're telling everyone we know how clever you are. Without a doubt, you're the best photographer I've ever used. And in my seventy-two years, I've tried plenty."

"I appreciate the kind words, but that designation belongs to my father."

"My late husband Arthur and I had several photos taken by him, and he was good. But you— you made my girlfriends and me feel so comfortable, we forgot about the camera. You caught us au naturel, which we all agree is a much more flattering look than any artificial pose."

"Wow. Thank you."

"I wouldn't have said it if it wasn't the truth. Good or bad, I always say what I mean."

"I'll bet that gets you into trouble."

"All the time. Along the way I've lost a few people I considered friends, even after I apologized for something I said. I'd rather offend someone than have to live with myself for holding back. With me, what you see is what you get."

How refreshing. "You're brave."

"I wasn't always this way. I used to be a people pleaser, saying and doing what I thought would make others happy without a thought for what I wanted. I made myself miserable and angry, and those I cared about paid the price."

"You, miserable? I'd never have guessed."

"I was. That's why my first two marriages failed. It took years of therapy before I wised up and started being myself. Then Arthur came along. He liked the real me. We had a wonderful marriage and were happy until the day he died."

"You're full of surprises. I had no idea you'd been married three times."

"Now you know. I'm telling you this because I sense you're also a people pleaser. You didn't ask for advice, but me being me, here it is. Don't stand in your father's shadow or anyone else's. You're fabulous all by yourself. Be who you are."

Be who you are.

The words resonated inside Grace.

In the bathroom again after the conversation ended, she mulled over Constance's advice while she finished the drawers. The woman had pinpointed what Grace hadn't realized. She'd spent her entire life pleasing Robert and to a lesser degree her mother. She still was, even though like Constance, doing so made her deeply unhappy.

The insight struck with stunning clarity. No more pleasing her father by hiding his secrets and wrongs.

It was time to be her real self.

That she could do this awed her, and something deep inside her heaved a sigh of relief. Feeling different already, she straightened her shoulders and studied her reflection in the bathroom mirror. The determined glint in her eyes pleased her. The knot that had been in her stomach since she'd discovered who Robert really was finally loosened, easing the guilt and fear that had made her life intolerable.

The real Grace wanted to tell Liam everything, even if the thought was a little scary. All right, a lot scary. He'd likely despise her. Bad enough her father had blackmailed Gil and ultimately caused his death. Worse, Liam would be furious that she'd hidden the truth from him.

Regardless, he had a right to know.

First, she'd talk to her mother. This instant.

She'd have a fit, but Grace couldn't let that stop her. Determined, she picked up her cell phone.

"I was just about to call you," her mother said. "We should talk. I know there's a ton of snow out there, but can you come over?"

"I would if I had my car. I went to the mall last night and had to leave it behind."

"I'm glad you didn't try to drive. Neither did I. My car is still parked in the employees' lot behind the hardware store. Crews are out clearing the roads, but getting to them all will take awhile."

"Then let's talk on the phone."

"How did you get home?" her mother asked.

Grace didn't even hesitate. "Liam gave me a ride. We ran into each other and ended up shopping together. We had a really good time. I want him back, Mom, although he may not take me. A few weeks ago, you suggested I start seeing him and hide the truth about Robert. I've decided to tell him instead. I'd like your blessing, but with or without it, I'm going to move forward."

Her mother started to say something but Grace wasn't finished. "Before you get upset, hear me out. I've been thinking about Robert—my promise to him and my fear of what others would think if they knew what he did, and my shame. Keeping his secrets is eating me alive. He's been holding both you and me hostage from the grave. Why should we let him control us? We didn't ruin his life—he did that all by himself—and we shouldn't let him ruin ours. I refuse to hide what he did anymore."

Speaking her truth felt good. Finished, she sat back and braced for her mother's outburst. To her surprise, Diane responded in a totally unexpected way.

"I came to the same decision this morning, and I agree one hundred percent. Your father's behavior doesn't reflect on us. Everything he did is on him."

Grace gaped at the phone. "Who are you, and what did you do with my mom?"

"That's an interesting story. Not long after the snow started last night, the manager decided to close the store. Mona and I were too nervous to drive, so we checked into the motel up the street."

"Is that where you are now?"

"I was until an hour ago. We both have today off and Mona drove me home—she has better tires. She's going to pick me up on the way to work tomorrow. I'll get my car then. Anyway, we shared a room and stayed up late talking. She told me about her ex-husband, awful things few people know, but she needed to talk about it. I listened without judging her, and she said I made her feel better.

"That sounded good to me, so I told her about your father. She didn't judge either. We gave each other big hugs. I slept like a baby. Today, I feel like I have a new lease on life."

"That's great, Mom. I want the same thing."

"You deserve that. I didn't mention the blackmail. No one should know about that until you talk to Liam."

"I agree. Once he knows, I doubt he'll want anything to do with me, but I can't rest until I've told him everything."

"I admire you, Grace. I wish I had your strength and courage."

"Thanks, Mom. I think we're both brave."

"Liam is bound to see that. If he cares about you, he'll forgive you."

With all her heart, Grace hoped that was true. "I think we should contact the police about the blackmail in person. If you don't want to come with me, I'll do it by myself."

"You'll have to go alone—I doubt I can get off work. When are you going to tell Liam?"

"Hopefully tonight." Although there was no guarantee he'd want to talk. "If I can't reach him, I'll leave a message and ask him to get in touch."

"I'm rooting for you, honey."

As soon as Grace showered and dressed, she phoned him.

12

F riday night poker games, open to anyone on Liam's shift, were a regular occurrence hosted at the home of a different crew member each week. Liam hadn't attended in a while. Rob was hosting tonight, which meant a thirty-minute drive, much of it on back roads. Kirkdale Road and the highway had been plowed and salted, along with many of the bigger residential streets, but not the narrower ones near Rob's. No prob, thanks to the Yukon.

If necessary, Liam would have walked. He needed to be with his crewmates and forget Grace.

About halfway to Rob's, the Bluetooth rang. Grace. Screw that. He wished her well, but he was off that roller coaster for good. He let it go to voice mail, then listened to the message.

"Hi, Liam. I need to tell you something. It's important."

The urgency in her voice was impossible to ignore. *Ah, hell.* He hit the redial button.

"What?"

If his growl intimidated her, she didn't let on. "Thanks for calling me back so quickly. Where are you?"

"On my way to a poker game. What's so important now that you couldn't say last night?"

"A lot. There are things I've kept from you, and until you know everything, my conscience won't leave me alone."

He pulled over and hit the break. "Say where and when."

"Now, and can you come here? I haven't picked up the minivan yet."

Never mind the poker game. "I'll be there in twenty."

GRACE CHECKED the time every few minutes while she waited for Liam. Still, when the security phone rang she nearly jumped out of her skin. She'd never been this anxious. She picked up the receiver and tried to speak. Only a rusty squeak came out.

"I'm here." Liam hung up.

She buzzed him in and minutes later, ushered him through her door. "Can I get you something to drink?"

"No, thanks." He dropped his coat on the piano bench, then leaned against the wall with his arms crossed and his infamous scowl firmly in place. "So talk."

His irritation didn't help and was only going to get worse. Grace's legs shook too much to support her. She dropped into the armchair and she hugged herself. Her hands were icy, cold enough to make her shiver, and her stomach... She feared she might throw up.

Channeling the courage her mother had praised her for, and Constance's advice to be herself, she went straight to the point. "Last night was fun. I enjoy being with you. I've missed that so much." She paused to draw a calming breath. "This isn't easy for me. I'm terrified, but in the spirit of being as open as I used to be, here goes. All I ask is that you let me finish before you comment."

She waited for his nod. "I don't know how to say this, so I'll start with the promise I made my father shortly before he died. He asked me to forgive him for his mistakes and to preserve his legacy. Without question I promised to do both. But if I'd known what those mistakes were, I..."

Her voice wobbled and she stuttered to a stop. Liam's raised eyebrows erased the scowl. Somehow that helped, and she explained about the gambling, her mother's forged signature, and secret debts. "You assumed my mother took a second job to keep busy. The real reason is, she needs the extra money to pay the second mortgage on the house. I'm paying the other bills."

"Even the loan shark? How did you pay him back?"

"I liquidated my savings, pawned the diamond stud earrings Robert gave me on my twenty-first birthday, and put off paying other bills, which ruined my credit. That's why I never bought chains for the minivan—I had no way of paying for them. I also lived on popcorn and ramen noodles for a while." Remembering, she made a face. "It was either that or lose the business."

"That sucks."

"Yes, and my mom and I were both so ashamed, we made a pact to not tell anyone."

"I wish you'd told me. I could've helped." He pushed away from the wall and started toward her.

If he touched her now, she'd chicken out before she finished. She held up her hand, warning him away. "There's more, and it's much, much worse. You may want to sit down." She waited until he was seated on the sofa. "I thought I'd uncovered all his secrets, but I was mistaken. One afternoon a few days later, I was sorting through his files when I came across an unmarked envelope. Inside were negatives I wish I'd never found."

Fighting the urge to look away, she forced herself to meet Liam's gaze. "They were of Gil and another man in a compromising position. I'm guessing they matched the pictures found after Gil's death. I don't know how my father knew him. All we could figure out is that he was apparently blackmailing Gil."

There—she'd told Liam everything.

Revulsion and shock drained his face of color. Grace swallowed, regret sharp and burning in her throat. "I should've told you a long time ago."

"Not just me, the police."

"I'm going to do that next. I thought you should know first."

"This is why you closed yourself off and ended our relationship—you didn't want me to find out."

His tone was mild but his unusual stillness and the subtle tic in his jaw warned her otherwise. He was livid and had a right to be.

He wasn't a violent man, yet she trembled all the same. "It was the only way forward that made sense. I couldn't tell you, Liam. I was—am—so ashamed. And scared."

She'd seen him upset, but never like this. Not even when he mentioned Joe. His expression indifferent, his eyes flat, as if she were someone he disliked and had dismissed. As if he no longer saw her.

A chill shuddered through her, penetrating

her soul. "You have no idea how sorry I am for hiding the truth from you."

Long, heavy silence.

"Say something," she pleaded.

After scrubbing his hand over his face several times, he stood. "I need to get out of here."

He collected his coat. Then he was gone.

13

Wrung out after an anguished night of crying and self-loathing, Grace texted Marguerite early Saturday morning and asked for a ride to the mall to pick up her car before they both had to go to work. She'd booked a full day of appointments and needed to get to the studio as soon as possible.

Her friend showed up in a great mood. "You'll never guess—Thursday, Zane called and invited me to lunch," she bubbled as she zoomed down the highway. The sky was gray, with the road virtually clear and snow piled high on the sides. "That was before the blizzard. Tonight, we're going out to dinner."

"That's great," Grace said, unable to summon a smile.

Marguerite sobered. "What happened?"

The full story tumbled out. When Grace finished, she slumped in the passenger seat. "Now both you and Liam know the whole ugly truth."

"I'm shocked. I always thought your dad was such a cool guy. I can't even imagine how you must feel."

"Pretty awful. I wish Liam was half as understanding as you."

"He wasn't?"

Grace shook her head. "He was beyond angry that instead of telling him the truth, I broke up with him. Looking back it seems so cowardly, but at the time... I tried to explain that I was too ashamed. I was scared, too. I don't think he listened to a word I said after I told him. Then he left." There went the tears. She swiped at her eyes and blew her nose. "I'd give anything to go back to when I first learned about it, and lay out the facts right then."

"You know that's impossible."

"I still wish I could." Regardless, she didn't regret that he finally knew. "I guess losing him is my penance for hiding the truth."

"Don't be so hard on yourself, Grace. You've had almost a year and a half to come to grips with a bunch of nasty surprises. Liam just found out. Give him time to process."

"You didn't see his face. The way he looked at me..." Remembering, she cringed. "He despises me, and I doubt he ever wants to see me again. I'd be furious if he'd done to me what I did to him."

"If I were Liam, I'd want to scream bloody murder and punch something."

"You're not helping."

"All I'm saying is, let him work through this. We both know he cares about you. He'll come around."

"That's what my mother said, but we all know the chances of that are about one in a zillion." Grace groaned. "The holiday party at Auntie's Place is this Thursday. How am I supposed to get through that? How will he?"

"As you always say, you'll survive by being the professional you are. How Liam behaves is up to him."

"That's what I hope, but I'm a total mess. After Robert's death, I convinced myself that I had to forget Liam. The truth is, I never did and doubt I ever will. I so want him back."

"Then suck it up and apologize again."

∾

"You look like hell," Rob commented when Liam arrived at the station well before breakfast Monday morning.

No kidding—he was still reeling from the bomb Grace had dropped on him Friday night. "You wouldn't believe it if I told you."

"Try me."

"Long story, and I need to stop at Rosemary's and pick up the breakfast sandwich I ordered."

Rob checked his watch. "We have plenty of time. I could use a coffee and a scone. I'll walk with you."

The day's gray cold suited Liam's dark mood. On the way, he filled his crewmate in. "That's the shit show I've been dealing with."

Rob looked like he'd sucked an extra sour lemon. "Effing unbelievable."

"What really fries me is that she didn't tell me until Friday night. She knows all the gory details about my past—my mom and Joe, that I lost both my parents within six months of each other, the disaster of my first marriage, the value I place on trust and honesty, the whole shtick. What did I get from her? A bunch of lies about her family. They seemed perfect and she let me believe it."

"Maybe she believed it too."

Liam pulled off his winter cap, ran his hand over his head, and put the cap back on. "I guess she did until her father passed. Once she found out about his shady secrets, she should've told me. That's what a committed relationship is based on, a partnership where a man and woman lean on each other and work out their problems together. She called it quits. That's what really galls me. I wonder if she ever cared."

"She cared—that much was obvious by the way she looked at you. Think about it, man. Her father dies and she finds out he's not the saint she thought he was. He gambled away all their money, took on a crap load of debt, lied to his wife and Grace, and resorted to blackmail, a criminal act. If he'd been caught, he'd have been sent to prison and fined a lot of money. I doubt his photography business would've survived either.

"If that's not bad enough, the man he black-mailed was a former firefighter, a decent guy and your mentor and friend, who happened to like men and women. Then to have Gil's possible suicide on his conscience... The whole thing sucks."

"Like I don't know that. The blackmail went down way before Grace and I met. If she'd told me, we could have dealt with it together." Liam shook his head. "Want to hear the kicker? I sensed that she'd pulled away because she was hiding something. I saw her mom once, and it was obvious she was doing the same thing. According to Grace, they made a pact not to tell anyone. Over the past few weeks I asked Grace about it more than once. She blamed her distance on grief and the need to learn how to run the photography studio."

The conversation stopped while Liam paid for his order and Rob bought his stuff.

As they headed back, his crewmate picked up where they'd left off. "I feel for you, but I can see why Grace did what she did. In her shoes, I'd have gone over the cliff. If my father lied and ruined people like Robert Camry? I don't know that I'd want that to get around—I'd be too ashamed. I'd sure as hell have second thoughts about going to the police, especially when both men involved in the blackmail are dead."

"All right, but my point is, you wouldn't avoid

the people you cared about. You and Jenny are divorced, but you'd still have told her."

Rob nodded.

"Because?"

"Besides the fact that she's the mother of our daughters, she's always shown good judgment and I'd want her advice. Even though we're divorced, I trust her."

"Bingo."

"Ah, now I get it. In your mind, Grace didn't trust you enough to confide in you."

"That's right." And damn, it stung.

"She and her mom had that agreement. Plus, maybe she was scared you'd break up with her if you found out what her father did."

"You know me better than that. Sure, I would've been upset, but we both know she had no control over what Robert did." Liam scoffed. "The pact she made with her mom shouldn't have included me. She never even gave me a chance to react, just dumped my ass. If that happened to you, you'd be outraged."

"Hey, at least she finally told you. I give her props for that. What's your next step? Gonna talk to her or throw in the towel?"

Liam scratched the back of his neck. "Hell if I know. I'm still trying to get my head around the whole mess."

"You still have feelings for her?"

"Yeah," he grumbled.

"Then ease up on her and have a serious talk."

"I'm too damn pissed off."

"Understandable." Rob slanted him a look. "Didn't you want to get rid of the tension between you and her before the holiday party?"

Which was in three days. "I don't see that happening now."

They reached the station. During breakfast, Liam filled in the rest of his crewmates. Like Rob, they shook their heads and sympathized—with Grace as much as him. Which didn't make him feel any better.

Twenty-four hours later, he was still steaming and still undecided what to do.

14

Marguerite was right, Grace decided. She needed to talk to Liam again, offer a new heartfelt apology, and ask for another chance. Determined, she rescheduled her Tuesday morning photo shoots and drove to the station.

A huge gamble. For all she knew, Liam was out fighting fires. Or he could refuse to see her, or throw her apology back in her face. At that daunting thought, she almost turned the minivan around. But if she wanted him back, she had to try. Surely if she was calm and heartfelt, he'd forgive her.

She timed her arrival for shortly after breakfast. Miranda, the woman who was always at the front desk, seemed surprised to see her. "It's been a long time," she greeted with a smile. "Are you here to talk about the holiday photo shoot at Auntie's Place? If so, no one bothered to inform me you were coming."

Grace shook her head. "Actually, I'm here to see Liam. Is he busy?"

"Let's find out." Miranda pressed the intercom button.

"Don't tell him it's me, okay?"

The woman's eyes widened. "All right."

Moments after she announced that Liam had a visitor, he strode through the secured door behind Miranda's desk and into the lobby where Grace waited. His eyes narrowed, but at least he didn't do an about-face and leave.

"Can I talk to you in private?" she said, sounding far calmer than she felt.

"Are there any meeting rooms available?" he asked Miranda.

"Take your pick." She buzzed them through the secured door.

"God knows what you're going to hit me with this time," Liam muttered.

Grace flinched, but for the sake of making things better, she didn't reply. Calm and sincere.

He ushered her into what looked like a classroom, with white boards attached to one wall, chairs neatly stacked at the back, and a standard folding table up front. Lifting a chair from the pile, he set it down, then strode to the other side of the table and stood there. Sullen, hands low on his hips.

If he meant to intimidate her, he was out of luck.

At almost a foot shorter than him, she wasn't

about to make herself even smaller by sitting down. Holding her head high, she placed her hands on the back of the chair. "I took the negatives to the police station yesterday and met with Officer Karen Scoville. I told her that my father had taken them, and that I believed he blackmailed Gil Booker."

Liam nodded, a positive sign. "You followed through."

She prickled, then reined in her irritation. "I meant what I said—the days of protecting my father's image and hiding his secrets are behind me. Talking with Officer Scoville was almost as big a relief as telling you, like shedding a fifty-pound weight from my shoulders. She said that they still had no proof of money exchanging hands, and that the statute of limitations on the blackmail has run out. The limit is three years, and—"

"Gil died five years ago."

"Yes. The officer promised to destroy the negatives."

A beat of silence, then a grudging, "If that's all, I should get back to work."

He wasn't making this easy. "Will you give me a few more minutes? I'm not finished."

She'd have preferred a scowl to his terse nod and blank expression, but at least he didn't leave. "I want to apologize again for not having the courage to tell you about this right away. In hindsight, I wish I hadn't made the pact of silence with my mom. I hated myself for keeping those secrets," she said. "But I never stopped caring about you."

"Could've fooled me. People who care about each other don't leave when things get tough. Whatever happens, they deal with their problems together, as partners in the relationship. It's called trust."

"Trust has nothing to do with this. I was ashamed, devastated, confused, grief-stricken... Feel free to stop me at any time."

"I don't fault you for any of that. What bothers me is that I was there for you, and you didn't come to me for help and support. That's not a partnership, it's running away."

He was right, she *had* run away. "I'm not running anymore."

He didn't appear to have heard her any more now than the other night. "Trust and honesty are everything to me. You knew that, yet you had so little faith in me, you assumed I'd leave. Dammit, Grace, that's insulting."

His voice had risen to a near yell. Fighting to remain calm, she swallowed. "I made a terrible mistake."

Totally closed off to her, he didn't give an inch. "You sure as hell did."

Her own temper rising, she snapped back at him. "You want the whole truth? Besides my shame, grief, and confusion, I saw your eyes go cold when you mentioned Joe. You made it clear you were unwilling to forgive him even after all these years. I was afraid you'd look at me like that and cut me out of your life. I was right."

"What do you expect me to do, take you back with open arms?" He snorted.

"No, but I hoped you'd hear me out. I drove all the way over here to explain and apologize for the second time, but like before, you ignored everything I said. What else am I supposed to do?"

"There's nothing left *to* do."

He'd made up his mind. That was that, then.

Grace gripped the back of the chair and managed to keep her chin up, but inside she crumpled. Still, she had to ask. "So we don't have a chance of getting back together?"

"I need to think about that. What's to stop you from running away the next time something unpleasant crops up?"

Struggling for a way to assure him she wouldn't, she didn't answer immediately.

Thumb and forefinger on his eyebrows, he glanced down and blew out a loud breath. "That's what I figured. I'll see you to the door."

DUE TO THE glut of appointments Grace had after rescheduling the morning, she stayed at the studio late. The last shoot of the evening ended at eight. Alone at last, she nibbled a granola bar.

She wasn't hungry, but with a ton of work to finish before morning—with Christmas in exactly two weeks, her clients couldn't afford to wait for their photos—maintaining her energy level was important.

She didn't have time to feel sorry for herself either, and wasn't that a good thing.

Determined to give her best to the job, she selected and framed the proofs for her clients. She was in the process of sending them off when her cell phone rang.

Ridiculously hopeful, she glanced at the screen. Marguerite, not Liam.

What had she expected? He wasn't going to call.

"Hi," she said when she answered.

"You sound really low."

"I'm tired and depressed. I showed up at the station this morning to talk to Liam. I bombed."

"Oh, no. What happened?"

"I said I was sorry. Instead of acknowledging my apology, he accused me of not trusting him. He yelled. I lost my temper and yelled back. It's over."

"So you had a fight. People do. It doesn't mean the end of anything."

"You weren't there." Suddenly cold, Grace rubbed her arms.

"I don't understand about the trust comment."

"Neither did I, so he explained. I should've told him about Robert instead of running away from our relationship. I agreed with him whole-heartedly and repeated how scared I was to tell him, but it didn't make any difference."

"You didn't say anything to me either, but I don't see what that has to do with trust. I admit, I was hurt—you and I have always been close. But you kinda had to keep your troubles private, and for good reasons. Heck, I have secrets too."

"Let me guess—you're writing a romance novel?"

Marguerite snorted. "I read them, I don't write them. This is something that happened in high school that I never told you. I got caught shoplifting."

"No way."

"It's true. Remember that Presidents' Day weekend when I visited Jennika in Portland? While I was there, I stole a dress from a department store."

"Why did you do that?"

"It was sexy and made me look older. It was also super expensive, way more than I could afford. So instead of leaving it in the fitting room, I put it in my shopping bag and left the department. I'd never done anything like that before and certainly haven't since. I got caught when I tried to exit the store. The dress was pricey enough to get me arrested and sent to juvenile detention."

"That's terrible!"

"It could've been, but the manager decided

not to press charges, thank God. He also contacted Jennika instead of my parents. For the rest
of the weekend, she yelled at me. I begged her
not to call Mom and Dad. She said she wouldn't
if I swore never to do it again."

"You didn't say a word about that to me. I'll
bet it had nothing to do with trust."

"You're right. I was embarrassed and worried
you'd judge me, and I was scared you wouldn't
want to be my friend anymore."

"Which makes perfect sense," Grace said.
"Why doesn't Liam get that?"

"Did you happen to mention that you want
him back?"

"Not in so many words. I asked if we have a
chance of getting back together."

"Good for you. What did he say?"

"That he needs to think about it. I'm not
holding my breath—he's always been hard-
headed. Once he makes up his mind about someone, he's done."

"Not where you're concerned," Marguerite
said. "Deep down, that man cares about you—I'd
stake my job on it. Do you think that talk you had
with him might have ended on a more positive
note if you'd said you loved him?"

"As hostile as he was? I would've died of humiliation on the spot. He doesn't want to be with
me because of my so-called lack of trust in him. If
my heartfelt apology didn't help, neither will
love."

"I disagree. Love can work miracles."

"Maybe in a fictional, happy-ever-after world."

"Convince him you love him and don't want to live without him—you'll see."

"What are you, a therapist?" Grace sighed. "Anyway, I took your advice this morning and nothing changed."

"It might, if you tell him how you really feel."

Grace couldn't help but be hopeful. "Do you really think so?"

"I'm no fortune teller, but don't you want to find out?"

"Supposing you're right," Grace mused. "How do I convince him that I can't bear the thought of spending my life without him?"

"You still have two days—you'll think of something."

15

Two hours before Grace was due at the holiday party, she steered the minivan through the traffic toward Auntie's Place. She wanted to talk to Liam before the families and kids showed up. This time, to bare her heart and soul, and if need be, sink to her knees and grovel, as distasteful as the thought was.

Whatever it took to convince him. The rest of her life depended on it.

She'd been on the road all of ten minutes when the sedan in front of her almost crossed the white line dividing the traffic, then veered in the other direction. The driver was likely texting or high.

Not wanting to get too close, she slowed down —mere moments before the sedan crashed into a metal barrier along the side of the road. Smoke poured from the hood of the car and vehicles in both directions braked to a stop. Along with several other drivers, Grace jumped out to help.

The man at the wheel of the sedan, a fifty-something male reeking of alcohol, had an ugly bump on his forehead and seemed dazed. He lay down on the ground and promptly began to snore. Someone called 911. Grace had an old blanket in her car and ran to get it. She covered him.

By the time the police finished and the medics drove the man to the hospital for a checkup, an hour had passed. A police officer directed traffic around the accident site, but progress was slow. So much for talking with Liam before the party. She might even be late. She sent him a hasty text.

Car accident. Be there when I can.

Once the officer beckoned her past the accident site, she hurried toward Auntie's Place.

FLANKED by a basketball court on one side and a garden patch on the other, Auntie's Place was a typical go-to hangout for kids. Besides a gym and study area with the usual computers and shelves of books and games, the sprawling, one-story building housed a kitchen and several offices.

For the last hour, Liam and the crew members who'd volunteered to decorate had transformed the gym into Christmas party central. Several Auntie's Place employees had stuffed goodie bags with holiday treats and trinkets, while others worked furiously in the kitchen to make the meal. The rest of Liam's crewmates, due to arrive shortly, had cleanup duty after the party.

Having changed into his costume, Liam emerged from the bathroom.

Rob grinned. "Lookin' good, Santa."

"Very funny. I feel ridiculous in this beard and padding."

"If you'd crack a smile, you could pass for jolly St. Nick himself."

Forget jolly. The first sharp bite of anger at Grace had faded some, leaving Liam with a hollow feeling inside. Nothing like betrayal to screw with a man's head. When she'd ended the relationship after her father's death, he'd been torn up and confused. This time felt worse, like he'd been run over by a fire truck.

Not the best state of mind for a guy playing Santa, but dammit, he refused to disappoint the kids and their families. He tried a grin. "Better?"

"Much."

"Good enough." The beard and wig were too warm, and so was the Santa hat. Liam took them and the round-rim glasses off for now and placed them on the "Santa" chair set aside for kids to sit on his lap and tell him what they wanted for Christmas.

Rob clapped him on the shoulder. "Our guests won't start arriving for at least forty minutes. You have time to talk to Grace and make up —if that's what you want."

"What I want and what is are two different animals. There's a little thing called trust that's missing. I can't have a serious relationship without it."

"No arguments there, and I agree, standards are important. But there are times when a guy ought to give a little. Grace screwed up, but she did the best she could at the time. Now she's trying to make it right. Instead of thumbing your nose at her apology, maybe you should accept it." Rob gestured at Nate. "Back me up on this, will you?"

"I'm with him," Nate said. "Your relationship isn't perfect—whose is?—but working out your problems together changes everything. Becca and I did that, and trust me, we both had plenty of baggage. Hell, we still do, but we're committed to each other. Knowing she has my back and I have hers, no matter what, has brought us closer. If we can make it work, so can you."

Both men had good points. Liam scratched the back of his neck. He had been pretty rigid about the trust thing, but did he really want—just then his cell phone signaled he had a text. He slid the phone from his pocket, glanced at the screen, and felt sick, almost as bad as he had when his mother had died. "Grace has been in a car accident."

Rob's jaw dropped. "Is she all right?"

"She didn't say, but I'm going to find out." He was calling her when another text arrived.

On my way—be there in ten.

Relief flooded him. "She must be okay—she's on her way."

Both his teammates exhaled loudly.

The rest of the crew had arrived, along with Captain Comings. They tromped inside, joking and ready for the evening ahead. The captain's phone rang. When he finished the call, he grinned. "Tony can't make it tonight. Summer's in labor."

Whoops broke out, everyone in high spirits.

The scare over Grace had set Liam straight. With complete clarity, he realized he wanted her back. He handed his secret Santa gifts to Nate. "Put these under the tree for me. I'm heading outside to wait for Grace."

Rob gave him a thumbs-up. Other guys called out, "Good luck," "Go for it," "About time." Liam couldn't agree more.

Outside was cold and already dark, and Liam stomped his feet to keep warm. At last, she pulled into the lot and parked at the side of the building, leaving the spaces in front for the families. He crossed the pavement to her minivan and opened her door.

Her eyes widened. "Liam."

Too emotional to speak, he reached in, unbuckled her seatbelt, pulled her out of the minivan, and looked her over carefully.

"What are you doing?" she asked.

"You were in a car accident. I'm checking you for injuries."

She gaped at him. "I wasn't involved in the accident. The driver in the car in front of me was drunk and had a collision. An aid car took him to the hospital. I'm sorry I didn't make myself clearer."

"Hey, as long as you're okay... I'm awful glad about that." He pulled her into a bear hug.

"I'm great now," she said when he let her go. She raised her eyebrows at him. "Nice Santa suit. It fits much better than the other one."

"Yeah." He tipped up her chin. "About the way we left things at the station the other day... Can we have a do-over?"

Her smile brightened the darkness. "Yes, but thanks to the accident, I'm a little pressed for time. I want to take 'before' shots of you and the crew, and I also need to set up so that I can capture the kids from the second they arrive. Let's talk later."

"For sure. Here's something for you to think about." He kissed her, then rested his forehead against hers and smiled. "I miss you, Gracie."

Her eyes filled. "Me too." Sniffling, she reached into the van and pulled the lever to open the rear lift gate. "I'd better take my gear inside."

Liam nodded. "I'll give you a hand and we'll bring it in together."

"I'd like that."

16

After a raucous few hours, the Auntie's Place party was winding down. Grace had taken tons of photos. Her favorites were of Liam and his elves, aka Owen, Max, and Ethan, in hats not unlike those of Constance and her group of widows, handing out the secret Santa gifts after the meal.

Lots of laughter, her own included. Liam's kiss and request for a do-over had restored the sense of optimism Robert had all but obliterated. She could hardly wait for them to talk.

Adam glanced at his phone, then tapped on his glass. "I have an announcement. My crewmate Tony Clark and his girlfriend Summer just became the proud parents of a little girl. They're calling her Elle, short for Noel. They also contacted a justice of the peace. They're getting married tonight, at the hospital."

Everyone was thrilled. If all went as Grace hoped, she'd soon meet Summer and little Elle.

Kids lined up to sit on Santa's lap and confide in him, and the elves handed out candy canes and foil-wrapped chocolates. Grace photographed that too. She wanted to talk to Santa herself, but waited until the children and their parents left, and the captain and the rest of the crew were congratulating themselves on a successful party.

Finished with his Santa duties, Liam started to pull off his hat and his fake hair and wig. "Wait —don't I get a turn?" she asked.

"Ho ho ho, of course," he said, returning to the chair and patting his knee.

She settled on his lap. "I need to talk to you, Santa."

"Have you been a good girl?"

"I was bad, and I truly am sorry."

"Tell Santa all about it."

"Keeping secrets from you is no fun," she said in a voice for his ears only. "I promise not to do it ever again, unless it's a surprise, like what I got you for Christmas."

He tugged on a lock of her hair. "You got me something? What is it?"

"I haven't bought anything yet, but if you play your cards right, I will."

"What do I have to do?" He peered at her over the funny gold-rimmed glasses perched on his nose.

"Give me another chance. You won't be sorry, I promise."

"I believe you. I'm not perfect either. There are times when I get locked into what I want, with no wiggle room. Like I did with you and the trust thing. If I ever get that way in the future, I expect you to call me on it and anything else that bothers you."

"As long as you do the same. That day at the station, you wondered if I'd run away again if something else bad happened. I hope and pray that I never have to face anything as awful again. But if I do, I promise I'll tell you immediately. I know you'll be there for me, no matter what. That's what trust is all about."

"You learn fast. I'll be there. Always."

Her heart full, she beamed at him. "To paraphrase the song, it's beginning to feel a lot like Christmas. I'm finally getting into the spirit—the first time in almost three years. I haven't put up my tree or decorated the apartment yet. I'd love for you to come over and help me."

"Sure. When are you thinking?"

"As soon as you have time."

"How about tonight? It's early yet and I'm not on cleanup duty."

Grace bit her lip. "Okay, but the apartment is kind of messy."

"I'm not planning to check out your housekeeping. I hope you have mistletoe."

"No, but I can pick some up on the way home."

"Never mind—we don't need mistletoe for

what I want. As soon as we get to your place, I'm going to take you to bed and ravish you." His eyes smoldered. "I wish we were alone right now."

She went weak with love and desire. "I trust you so much that I'm going to share something else I've never told you."

"Okay," he said, looking wary.

"It's nothing bad. I love you, Liam Gibson, and I really, really want us to be a couple again."

A slow grin spread across his face. "That's good, because I love you too. Consider us back together. My grandpa will be so happy. This is what he wants for Christmas."

"Aww, that's so sweet. I can't wait to see him again."

"He feels the same about you. I feel so fantastic right now, I might even call Joe."

"The Joe you won't speak to?"

Liam nodded. "I've had enough of holding grudges to last two lifetimes."

"That's amazing, Liam. Have I told you how much I love you?"

"Yeah, but I don't think I'll ever get tired of hearing it."

They smiled at each other.

"How do you think your mom will feel about this?" he asked.

"She'll be thrilled. The four of us should spend Christmas together."

"Great minds think alike. Let's do it. Your place or mine?"

"Quit making moony eyes at her and kiss her," Rafe called out from the other side of the room.

Liam did.

THE END

THANK you for letting me share my stories with you!

IF YOU ENJOYED **MR. DECEMBER,** help others find this book by recommending it to your friends and by writing a review. If you would like to know when my next release is available and other fun stuff, sign up for my newsletter here: www.annroth.net

THERE ARE 10 sexy firefighter books planned for the **Heroes of Rogue Valley: Calendar Guys**

OTHER BOOKS:
Halo Island:
All I Want for Christmas
The Pilot's Woman
Ooh, Baby!

. . .

ANN ROTH CLASSICS:
  Father of the Year
  A Place to Belong
  My Sisters
  Another Life

VISIT ME AT FACEBOOK FACEBOOK.COM/ANN-ROTHAUTHORPAGE
  Follow me on Twitter @Ann_Roth
  Follow me on Instagram annrothauthor
  Email me at ann@annroth.net
  Visit my website www.annroth.net

THANKS, and until next time,
  Ann

ALSO BY ANN ROTH

ABOUT THE AUTHOR

Ann Roth is an award-winning author of 40-plus contemporary romance and women's fiction novels, as well as novellas and numerous short stories. Her first novel was published in 2000 by Harlequin Special Edition and was nominated by *Romantic Times* as best first book. Ann lives with the love of her life in the Greater Seattle area and enjoys creating flawed characters and putting them in challenging situations that help them grow and ultimately find love— whether or not they're looking for it.

Find out about new releases!
Sign up for my newsletter

Or visit my website www.annroth.net